SCRATCH

...an erotic tale...

By

Celeste Celeste

SCRATCH …an erotic tale…

Cover Art by

Monique Ward, On The Map Media

Edited by

Valerie Yager

CONTENTS

Prologue   page 7

Chapter 1   page 9

Chapter 2   page 17

Chapter 3   page 25

Chapter 4   page 35

Chapter 5   page 51

Chapter 6   page 71

Chapter 7   page 79

Chapter 8   page 105

Chapter 9   page 119

Chapter 10   page 123

Epilogue   page 135

6

Prologue

Everything slowed down.

I closed my eyes and tried to blink away the reality in front of me, I grabbed the frame of the door for stability. I felt weak in my knees. Never in a million years would I have thought things would turn out this way.

In no way am I claiming victim, because I know what I've done. I mean, that is why we were here, and I was trying to make it right. I knew we had a serious problem and I was ready to face it and work towards a resolution to save my marriage.

I thought I had it all figured out. I'd confess, he'd forgive me and recognize all the things he didn't do, all my needs he didn't fulfill and make it right, because he didn't want to lose me.

I was his wife, the mother of his children.

I was not prepared for this. I was not able to formulate enough thought to say a word. As I stood there, I was faced with the realization that the man I was trying to convince to stay was already gone.

I starred directly into her face with rage burning through my skin.

I tried to make a rational decision. I tried to think this situation through.

Just so you're clear I'm from the streets, the very bottom, I'd educated myself and sought out a different life style. I married well and never had to look back.

I guess that old saying was true, you can take the girl out the hood......but you can't take the hood out the girl. It's like the devil himself was begging me to show these two what I was made of.

I slowly took two steps into the room, closed and locked the door behind me. I grabbed the large vase of flowers on the table by the door; *my husband had probably bought them any fucking ways*. I tossed the entire thing across the room causing a large crash with the shattering of the glass.

They were lost in their own moment of shock, but I had their attention now!

On the other side of the door I could hear a frantic voice speaking to a 911 dispatcher. I didn't give a fuck, they would sure need them, and the way I saw it, they still had to get here and by then, I'd have my answers.

Chapter 1

It was 10:00 am sharp when we sat down for breakfast on Christmas morning. I placed the napkin in my lap and looked around the table.

We were preparing to say grace and bless the food.

After breakfast we'd go into the family room and finally allow the children to open their gifts.

They were tortured every year, forced to sit through a formal breakfast before being able to enjoy Christmas morning.

Following that the adults would have coffee and exchange gifts.

In the box with the shiny wrapping would be my amazingly wonderful gift; another fucking bracelet.

I must have a million bracelets, baguette fucking diamonds, round fucking diamonds, and even diamond fucking clusters! Who needed that many bracelets? I only had two arms!

I was so over my entire life.

Everything was the same routine day in and day out, year in and year out. I know exactly what is going to happen for the rest of my life right now and I am so over it!

I felt like Rose from the Titanic. I was expected to stay in this unhappy place because of what it could afford me.

"That man provides you with a wonderful life!" Dawn said.

Dawn is my best and only friend. I have no family in the state in which I live and I appreciate having someone in my life other than his family, but sometimes I swear she just didn't get it.

"Style" I inserted.

"What are you talking about?"

"Style Dawn, he provides a wonderful life-style, but he does not give me life, two very different things! A woman wants to feel like silk, and it is a man's job to make her feel that way."

"Well shit can't you just buy some silk pajamas or a silk sheet set and roll around in that?" Dawn laughed, but I didn't think she was funny at all, but I did get her way of thinking. Like Rose's mother in Titanic she would do anything to keep from going back to a life of poverty including disregarding her daughter's feelings for fortune.

Dawn was a single mother to one son and in order to give him a decent life she had to work two jobs.

From her vantage point all she seen were the benefits of having a wealthy man and assumed she would be able to deal with whatever else came with that.

I felt that way once before too, but that was about 8 years ago and since then I have been floating through existence letting life just pass me by.

I looked around the room at all of his family; they actually seemed to be enjoying the festivities. His mom, THE Mrs. Jones, as I was instructed to call her, came to visit every year. Thankfully she didn't come over too much. She only lived in the neighboring city, but every year for Christmas it was their tradition that they would all stay together.

She was a lovely woman, widowed a few years back when Sean's father died; she cherished her son and adored our two boys, Sean Jr. who was 7 and the baby Sammy, who was 5. She was poised and straight forward; I could certainly see where his structure came from because Mrs. Jones didn't play!

Mr. and Mrs. Jones only had two children, Sean was the baby, and his mother's favorite if you ask me. Alicia, his sister, was in attendance along with her husband John and their 9 year old son Aaron. Alicia and John were working on reconciling their marriage after their third divorce attempt. I guess they had an on again off again type of marriage.

Then there was my friend Dawn and her son Michael who was 5.

It was great for the boys growing up together and spending the holidays together every year.

We had a very large home and there was more than enough room for everyone. High vaulted ceilings, a chef's kitchen and a huge backyard for our boys. My husband provided a very secure, stable and traditional life for me. An entirely different social class from where I come from, probably why none of my family is here now, I left them and that lifestyle long ago and never really looked back.

Why wasn't I happy?

For me it was clear, my husband didn't make me happy. Our sex life was so basic and routine I could accurately predict the number of strokes before his orgasm. I could call out the positions in which we'd have sex and the order in which we'd have them. Here's what I didn't know; the last time my husband said I was beautiful, or the last time his lips touched mine, or the last time I actually climaxed from having sex with him, or the last time he hugged me, or the last time he walked past me and smacked my ass, or the last time he looked at me with lust in his eyes.

My husband would walk into the room, see me crying and sigh heavily at the thought of having to deal with the emotion of a woman. He could care less what the situation was, the fact that he had to be bothered with it was enough to frustrate him.

When my father died two years ago from cancer I didn't get so much as a hug to comfort me. He simply asked would I be attending the funeral. I looked at him like he had 3 eyes to which he replied, *people die Mariah, you go pay your respects and move forward, let me know what you plan to do so I can arrange for my mother to watch the boys.* He placed his hand on my shoulder and squeezed it gently. I am assuming as a sign of affection and walked away, never mentioning it again.

It's so hard to get people to understand when all they see is what is on the exterior.

"Mariah" my husband was calling my name.

"Yes Love?"

"Your gift," he passed me the shiny box that I already knew was mine. I opened the box and inside was, drum roll please, a bracelet.

"Thank you Love" I tried to muster up a smile. Dawn looked at me, with a sharp look, like she expected me to say more, when I didn't she jumped in.

"Sean you are soooo generous, look at that bracelet! How many karats is this?" she took the box from my hand as she and the rest of the room admired the bracelet, I tuned all of them out because I honestly didn't care to pretend at the moment.

I was so sick of this! How do you tell a man as arrogant as him that you are not happy?

"Let me see this bracelet," John took the box from Dawns hand, "O-K, I see you! Don't be trying to make me look bad Bro."

He certainly didn't need any assistance in that department; he was doing a fine job on his own.

I looked around the room as they all contributed to his ego. Everyone around him seemed to bow down and worship him. He was constantly praised for his accomplishments in life and the way he provided for his family.

Mariah is so lucky, they'd say.

I wonder if they knew Mariah has been faking orgasms for years! I wonder if they knew that Mariah fantasized about almost every man she seen because she was so starved for affection at home.

My situation was the classic 80 20 rule, which is probably why I was still here. My husband was an amazing man and provider but he was a horrible lover and that left me with an undeniable itch.

"Give me my present, thank you very much" I took the box from Dawn, trying to get back in the moment and not allow myself to drift away with my thoughts.

That was something Sean hated, I couldn't tell him what I was really thinking so he assumed I was daydreaming and not paying attention to anything, what he didn't know is I was indeed daydreaming but about another life that didn't include him.

I placed my hand over his on the arm of the sofa and caressed it as I mouthed the words thank you to him. He smiled and nodded like he was the man, if he only knew.

"I have a little headache Love, I am going to put a load of clothes in the wash and take a quick nap" I walked away before he or anyone could protest.

I had had enough of this morning. I'd be back in a few hours to set up for dinner and they'd be right there watching the game. *They'll be fine*, I thought.

In the laundry room I found a huge mess, clothes everywhere. I think my house guests assumed we had a maid.

Sean's family had stayed the past three nights, as they do every Christmas, and instead of taking their dirty laundry home, as normal people did, they piled it here for me to do!

I started separating the clothes and checking pockets to make sure the boys didn't leave any gum or crayons in their pockets when a business card fell to the floor.

Yolanda Young, Couples Counselor, uh-oh, trouble in paradise! I laughed, wondering if Sean's sister was leaving her cheating ass husband, again. One could never be too sure with those two.

I placed the card on a shelf and continued separating clothes, before loading the wash machine. I had my own issues to worry about, whatever was going on between Alicia and John was their business.

I looked in on the boys before heading upstairs; they were entertaining themselves with Jr.'s new PS4. I loved my sons and wanted nothing more than for them then to be raised with their father; I would stay and make this work, for them I had to at least try.

CHAPTER 2

It was another sleepless night for me. I tossed and turned the entire night.

I had been suffering from insomnia for some time. I didn't have an issue falling asleep; it was staying asleep.

I longed for my husband's deep stroke to wear my body out and put me back to sleep, but that would be like getting water from a rock.

I looked over at his sleeping body and sighed heavily.

Fuck it, I thought to myself, as I began to rub his muscular arms.

He was so sexy to me and I was still very much attracted to him. I loved the way he looked down to the way he smelled, too bad he wasn't that attracted to me, and if he was, he's never shown it.

When rubbing his arm didn't cause a stir, I turned my back to him and arched my ass firmly against his groin, grinding against his dick.

I could 'feel' his manhood responding to my advance, but he still remained motionless.

I knew he was awake, I was the heavier sleeper of the two of us and he always complained my tossing and turning disturbed him.

This was the shit right here! He knew I wanted to have sex with him, but he would ignore me or down right deny me. My own fucking husband!

I had gone for so many years not being pleased sexually that my sex drive had decreased drastically. I used to want sex on a daily basis, now after years of denial, I'd settle for once a week.

I did not think there was another woman in the entire world faced with this same issue.

What husband denies his wife sex?

I continued to caress his smooth skin, wondering why he doesn't love me.

Maybe love wasn't the right word, because I was sure that he loved me. For all the years that we have been together, I have never felt as if he was cheating, nor has he ever not come home. One would think with sexual issues, the culprit is usually another woman, but Sean displayed no signs of cheating other than our lack of sex.

I think I would rather he cheat, at least that way I would know why!

I just wanted to know why he was no longer attracted to me, for years I carried this weight, feeling insufficient.

I was a lady, I was his lady and I needed to be treated as such!

I found myself getting upset and frustrated, the itch was becoming uncontrollable, and soon enough I'd have to give in and scratch.

Sean moaned in his sleep.

"Daddy" I whispered in his ear.

He pretended not to hear me.

"Daddddddyyyy" I repeated in my sexy voice.

He turned from his side onto his back, "You alright?" he asked, eyes still closed.

I scooted closer to him, "....yes, I want you to wake up and help me get back to sleep Daddy," I continued kissing his arm and chest.

I took his hand and placed it on my precious petal, it was moist and eager for his arrival....but again no response. Not a single word, pissed I turned to my side, giving him my back and faced the door to our master bathroom.

This was the same situation that replayed every time we would have sex.

I come on to him, he ignores me. I huff and puff and turn my back to him. He spoons me from behind, fucks me like a robot, cums eight minutes later, washes up and within 10 minutes he's back to sleep like it never happened.

When I felt him inserting himself into me from the side, I knew it was time for our well-rehearsed mundane, sexual encounter.

He was so big and thick; I almost came from the feeling of him sliding that long pole inside of me alone. Feeling him slowly stretch my ways turned me on.

I hated that he felt so good. After all the years of rejection and being deprived of sex, he still turned me on and I wished that wasn't the case. I still yearned for my husband's touch.

His stroke picked up and he began to get his rhythm, I wanted to moan in pleasure and tell him that this pussy belonged to him, but he wasn't in to sex talk.

As a matter of fact, he wasn't into foreplay before sex, talking during sex or cuddling after sex.

In the beginning of our relationship I would tell him to fuck me harder, I'd ask him did he love the way my juicy pussy was sliding up and down his dick, never one reply, eventually I felt awkward so I stopped.

The no oral sex was a major bummer as well. I could suck and slurp and damn near swallow his dick and he wouldn't even mumble a word.

I know he enjoyed it because his toes would curl, but it was like he refused to give me the satisfaction of knowing that I was pleasing him. I often wondered if it was a control thing.

We were four minutes into it, the halfway mark. He was pounding away causing my ass cheeks to ripple with every stroke.

He felt so good inside of me I wanted to scream. I wanted him to kiss my neck, bite my ear, and make me look into his eyes as we climaxed together.

I wanted passion!

I assume he felt good as well. Under the circumstances one could never be sure.

Around the six minute mark he turned me over on my stomach. I arched my pretty round brown ass in the air as he began serving the best back shots he could pitch. I caught every single one too, pound for pound, throwing it back trying to get a reaction out of him......only to receive nothing.

Any minute now his stroke would get shorter, quicker and his legs would stiffen up, he would then pull out of me and cum all over my ass like I was some side chick.

My husband had never cum inside of me. When I got pregnant with both of the boys we learned it was from pre-cum. The doctor had to explain that to Sean after we returned to get the paternity results that we took for not one but both of our sons! Bastard.

He threw me a cold wash cloth to clean myself off, as he proceeded to wash all the remnants of my love down the drain.

Two minutes later he'd climb back into bed, careful to stay on 'his side', because cuddling was a game he didn't play. He'd be asleep in thirty seconds, but not before he giving me his signature look, or maybe it was a gesture, regardless, to me it was interpreted as, *damn are you happy now*, as if he did me a favor!

I would lie in bed, for hours, just thinking...probably more often than I should have.

I was 29 years old and this was my life, big car, even bigger house, wealthy husband, healthy boys and miserable on the inside. I didn't want to walk away from this beautiful family I'd built, but I didn't think I could stay either, not without some type of resolution.

Why did he stay?

I couldn't understand the dynamic of my household any longer. He didn't seem happy with me, but didn't seem to want to be without me either; it was like he wanted me there to be miserable.

He had it all, all the money was his, all the property; his. I would literally have nowhere to go if I left this man and would probably find myself on Dawn's couch, he would never let the boys live there even if it was temporary. I had somehow isolated myself from my entire family and found myself with no one to lean on. I had Dawn but she was a single Mom who lived in income-based housing so to her, I was living the dream. She was unable to relate and did not serve as a good confidant for the darker side of my marriage, the part no one knew about.

When Sean and I initially got together it was great, we were young and having fun, but as soon as I had Jr. things gradually changed and from that point forward I remember that annoying itch always being just outside of Sean's reach, leaving me frustrated and still itching.

It was just this one little thing, this single issue that was standing in the way of my happiness.

A few years ago I started fantasizing about another man coming in and picking up all the slack Sean left behind. Yes, I'd contemplated an affair, that way I could just get the sex I needed and still have the rest of my life at home, but who was I kidding, I barely had friends, let alone someone willing to sleep around with someone else's wife. Who wants to be a part of a messy love triangle? No-one had time for that, so I suffered in silence.

Funny, I had literally, always told my boys to try to resist itching, because once they'd start scratching it's even harder to stop, scratching only leaves punctured skin and scars.

Well I had been resisting for 7 years, 7 long years, fighting this urge............

Chapter 3

I had been telling Sean for weeks that I believed the car needed new brakes.

Every time I mentioned it, he seemed to ignore me or be bothered with the subject all together. I was so tired of his shit and so near my breaking point that everything ended in an argument in our home for the past few weeks even a question as simple as what do you want for dinner.

This particular day I was enraged!

I stormed in the house Saturday afternoon after leaving the mall.

He was on the sofa watching college football drinking a beer, enjoying his down time, but I didn't give not one single fuck!

"Sean I mentioned the brakes to you over and over, there is something wrong with my car! I was driving home today and nearly crashed twice! I mean you are the man of this house, I get you don't want to have sex with me but I didn't know you were abandoning all your manly duties in this house!"

If looks could kill I would have been deceased because the daggers he shot at me were lethal.

"Every single thing is an issue with you!" He stood up and snatched the keys out of my hand and went outside.

I was always viewed as the culprit no matter what I did. I mentioned this car to him two months ago, and every week from then forward. I should have been the one pissed! Did he want me to crash and die?

I walked outside behind him, just as annoyed as he was!

"Get in" he ordered as I walked outside.

We couldn't have been going far since the boys were still inside and we never left them home unattended.

I suggested 4 weeks ago that he at least drive the car around the corner so he could see what Iwas referring to. I guess he was finally going to drive my car to help figure out the issue.
I am not a man or a mechanic yet I was made to feel wrong for asking my husband for assistance with this.

"Thank you," I said sarcastically from the passenger seat.

We drove around the block twice in complete silence, before finally pulling back into our driveway.

"So?" I asked rolling my neck. He hated 'ghetto gestures' as he would call them,

"Look I have no clue what is wrong with this car, I don't drive it you do, sorry I am not a greasy mechanic who can fix your plumbing and your car, but I did fix your life. I am a high paid executive who gave you a life you could only dream of. I work every day while you parade around town shopping and getting your nails done and whining about everything else! How could a girl who comes from so little want so much? Are you that helpless, I thought girls from the hood were survivors," he laughed, "you are one of the neediest women I have ever met!"

I stood there in shock, but not really because no matter what the issue was it was always my fault.

He wasn't done yet, "You have access to not one, not two, but three credit cards that have no limit and you need me to help you do everything! Take the car to the mechanic Mariah, or do you need me to do that for you too? Should I call in to work and take the car or can you peel yourself from those stupid ignorant reality shows you watch on demand all day? I mean if we can live off of your paycheck, I'd gladly stay at home to be at your beck and call. Oh but wait, you don't have a paycheck do you?

"Fuck you Sean!" I was so tired of his verbal abuse.

"I'll pass, no thanks" he tossed me my keys and pushed pass me into the house.

I sat on the porch and cried.

Why was I holding onto this marriage? This man was clearly no longer in love with me and took every opportunity he could to remind me of where I came from and what he does for me and how he changed my life. I was so tired of this life, but who was I kidding? Where was I going?

I didn't know but for right now I was going for a walk.

I thought about a lot during that walk, my mom, how she was addicted to drugs my entire life, my father whom I never met, how I longed for an escape out of poverty, how I studied so hard to earn my degree so I could get a good job and afford a better life for myself, how I had always wanted to have a wealthy husband and have 2 sons, how I thought when I met Sean he was my dream come true. How overnight I had all the things I had ever dreamed of.

I began to question did I even love my husband or was it the lifestyle that he was able to afford me that I was in love with. Were we ever friends? Or did I fit the description of his ideal woman as he fit perfectly into my vision of what I wanted? This marriage was going downhill and fast and I had no clue what my next move should be.

I wasn't like Dawn. I mean hats off to her but it wasn't my ideal of life. I honestly was not ready to give up my lap of luxury and be a single parent struggling to make ends meet. Sean would never allow his boys to live under certain conditions and I could not be sure that he wouldn't try to seek full custody if I tried to leave. Maybe I would let him take his sons, and I could move on alone, almost like hitting the reset button and getting another chance to make my life right, the way I want it to be.

I must have been losing my mind, I felt myself slipping, contemplating letting Sean take my boys, over my dead fucking body!

We lived in a suburb but I had walked quite a distance and was now in the parking lot of a shopping center. I walked into a small coffee shop and ordered bottled water. I was in such a zone that I completely forgot that I had just left home; I didn't have my purse, my wallet or any cash on me at all.

"Ok ma'am, that'll be $2.19." the bubbly cashier stated, smiling through her braced teeth.

"Shit" I mumbled when I realized that I didn't have any money. How the hell was I supposed to leave my husband when I couldn't even afford bottled water without his credit card!

"I'm sorry, I must have left my wallet I fumbled checking all of my pockets again although I already knew they were empty. I felt a little embarrassed especially when the guy inline behind me cleared his throat as if I was taking too long.

"I'm sorry, let me put this back" I said reaching for the water from the cashier.

"I got it"

The cashier, whose name tag read 'Jenny' and I both looked to see who had offered to hydrate my body by purchasing me the bottled water.

6 feet and 2 inches in the air stood who would later be introduced as Aurel.

I must have stood there starring because cute little Jenny said "Anything else guys?" I was stuck.

"Yes, add 5 number three's" referring to lottery tickets, "and I have a Pepsi here."

I stood to the side and he paid Jenny and passed me my water.

"Thank you" I said feeling awkward and shy at the same time.

"You are very welcome beautiful"

No one had called me beautiful in a long time

"Thank you again," I said head down, knowing that my face was red from blushing.

"What's your name?"

I heard him but was unable to answer, his cologne had me in a trance and then he smiled revealing two of the deepest dimples I'd ever seen. I know my face got red because I could feel the warmth.

"Um, Riah, I mean Mariah, my name is Mariah but people call me Riah." I was stumbling all over my words acting like a school girl. *Get it together chick*, I told myself.

"Hey Riri my name is Aurel but you can call me Rell."

"Who said I was going to call you?" Wait! Was I flirting with this stranger a few blocks from my home? Out in public??

"You are going to call me when you get home cause I want my $3 back!" We laughed and I found my hand on his arm. I immediately removed it. What was I doing?

"Hold up, that water was $2.19!" I was trying not to be so awkward.

"Oh that's interest Riri, ain't nothing in this world free, but I will settle for your number." He smiled and those deep dimples appeared, again. *Mmmmmmmm.*

Number? Reality had kicked in by now and I knew there was no way I was giving this man my number.

"I am sorry Rell, but I have a husband," I said too quickly.

"Well you look like you need a better one."

He looked me up and down.

I didn't realize until now that I had on house shoes, I had fly a way's all over my head because of my long walk and to top it all off I didn't even have $2 in my pocket, I guess I was looking a tad rough. I felt embarrassed.

"I don't live to far away from here, I said instantly regretting that. I didn't want some strange man lurking in my neighborhood trying to find me. I just took a walk and got a little caught up and wandered too far.

"What has your mind so distracted?"

I looked at him but didn't respond. I couldn't.

There was something so inviting about him. God this man was attractive.

"Well can I give you a ride Riri, drop you back off at home?" he looked genuinely concerned and then he smiled and those dimples came back.

"My um, husband, probably wouldn't be ok with that, he must be looking for me so I should start heading back. It was nice to meet you, uh, uummm..."

"Rell"

"Yes! Rell. Thank you again for the water."

I walked away, I know it seemed rude but I had to, trust me.

Rell watched me as I walked away.

I know because when I looked back he waved still standing in the same spot I had left him in. I waved back and kept it pushing not wanting him to think that I wanted to be pursued any further.

I had to get my ass home, because I know Sean was probably worried sick, it had been 2 hours!

I started my hike back home, looking back every so often to make certain I wasn't being followed.

When I got to the house he was right on the couch watching sport center like he didn't have a care in the world.

I had prepared what I would tell him when I walked in the door as he badgered me about my whereabouts and lectured me on how unsafe it was to walk off with no id, no phone and no money, but he didn't say a word, he just turned the TV up which I interpreted that as 'do not bug me.'

He didn't give a damn about me or my damn safety.

Well fuck him too, I thought as I went to check on my boys.

They were rough housing in the garage playing air hockey, totally oblivious to the war of roses going on in our home.

I backed out and quietly closed the door leaving them to enjoy their Saturday.

CHAPTER 4

It was Valentine's Day and tonight I planned to try something different with my husband.

I wanted to make up. We hadn't said much to each other since last weekend when we fought about my car.

I desperately needed him to know the way I needed to be touched. He had no idea that I enjoyed rough sex or even that I secretly wanted to try anal sex. I could just never get the courage to tell him. I needed him to take this pussy like he owned it, because he did!

My husband was going to learn how to fuck me tonight, and I was going to teach him.

I pulled my car into a parking spot outside of the food court at the mall. I parked as far away as possible; the extra walking was good exercise, exercise that contributed to my plump ass that seemed to grab everyone's attention, with the exception of Sean of course.

I stopped in Victoria's Secret and immediately found a cute baby pink satin nightie with the matching robe.

It was cute, but the naughty side of me wanted something a little.....naughtier. I quickly headed to the line to make my purchase then headed over to Fredericks of Hollywood for sexier attire.

I was on a mission to find the most seductive, inappropriate lingerie possible. I scanned through the items on display and found myself torn between a black one piece with what looked like tiger tears along the sides and a money green lace bodysuit.

"I like the green one better."

I turned around to find a young man with a mouth full of gold teeth staring at me through barely opened eyes.

He smelled like marijuana.

Too bad, he was kind of cute too, but I'd never disrespect Sean with a dope boy.

"Do you really?" I asked, not really sure why. Any attention was better than no attention I guess.

"Yeah babe, and you got it, damn, all that ass! Shit, I'd buy you everything in this bitch and have you model it for me all day."

"Is that right?"

"Yeah lil' Mama, that's right. M-M-Mmmm!" He was undressing me with his chinky eyes.

He wasn't my type at all, I thought, turning to admire my reflection in the mirror. I did like the way the green looked against my skin.

'Smokey' was now standing behind me, blatantly starring at my ass.

"My husband should like this," I turned to face him, emphasizing on the word husband.

"Damn, ok Mama. Yo husband sho is a lucky man, you got the fattest ass I've ev......"

"Ok, thank you, nice meeting you- gotta go."

I damn near ran to the register trying to get away from 'Smokey". What the hell was he doing in the lingerie store anyway?

I made my purchase and exited the mall as quickly as possible, then headed to the liquor store to get a bottle of vodka. I had wine at home and Sean had his beer, but tonight, I planned to step outside of that boring ass box he had us trapped in.

Dawn picked up the boys from school that evening and was on her way to my house to get an overnight bag for them.

Dawn may have lived in low-income housing but that was the sacrifice she made to give her son a better education. Our boys went to the same private school, which was a god-send when I needed her help with pick up and vice versa.

I rushed home to hop in the shower.

Dawn arrived 10 minutes later with the boys.

"MOM! Me and Sean Junior and Aunty Dawn are hereeee!"

"Ok baby boy", I said coming down the stairs, "Hey Sammy, I missed you all day!"

I kissed all over his face as Sean Jr. went to the fridge for a drink.

"Excuse me Mister! Hello to you too! Did you wash your hands before going into my fridge?"

"Hi Mother. I know, I know..." He closed the fridge and walked to the guest bathroom to wash his hands.

"Hey Boo." I kissed Dawns cheek.

"What's up Girl?" She asked cheerful as always.

"Thanks for taking the boys for me. I plan on getting it popping tonight with Sean's boring ass! Where is Mikey?" I said, just realizing that her son Mike wasn't with the group.

"He is in the car asleep, I didn't want to wake him, plus we will be in and out so...." She grabbed bottled water from the fridge.

I started to ask her did she wash her hands before going in my damn fridge, but I decided against that.

"You better bust it wide open for Sean too! Get out the red bulbs and rock his world girl, let him know how grateful you are for all of this."

She put her hands in the air.

"Girl if he was my man,,,,,"

"We know, 'you'd wait on him hand and foot'!" I cut her ass off, I hate when she referenced what she would do to my husband if he was hers, cause he wasn't! "But you're not with him, so don't worry about it and don't be sweating my technique! After tonight the flame will be reignited, bet that!"

"Oooowwww!" We high fived. "Let me see what you picked out real quick!"

"I don't have time girl, he is on his way home and ya'll gotta get gone!"

"Alright, alright. Come on boys! We are going bowling, so there!"

My boys loved Dawn and I truly appreciated her at times like these, but for now I needed them all to disappear.

After seeing my boys off and realizing I was running out of time I decided to crack open the bottle of vodka I had picked up earlier.

I needed to set the mood, so I poured myself a shot, and then another one.

Why the hell am I so nervous? *This is my husband*, I thought to myself.

That was the problem, part of me knew he wouldn't be a willing participant in the night's festivities, but I had to try and it was too late to back out now, so I continued to get ready for my evening.

Over the next fifteen minutes I had seductively scented candles placed throughout the house, and a trail of red rose petals leading to the living room where it would be, 'going down'.

I had strawberries, whipped cream, chocolate and lubricant.

I needed my world rocked and I was tired of yearning for something I should have been getting at home.

I was upstairs finishing my makeup when I heard his car pull into the driveway.

I took one last look in the mirror. I decided on the more reserved pink piece. This was my first time and Sean was very conservative so I decided subtle was the best approach.

My skin shimmered against the pale pink satin fabric. I straightened my shoulder length hair and pinned the side up, and then took it down, and then pinned it up again. I was so nervous. I had applied a full face of makeup and hoped to smear every bit of the Mac products that I wore all over my man. I put on my heels and hurried down to greet my Husband.

I was nice and tipsy at this point. I had been listening to R. Kelley's sexy ass for the past hour talk about all the ways he pleased women and I was ready for my man to do the same for me.

Unable to decide if I wanted to spread out across the sofa, or greet him at the door, I ran into to the guest bathroom when I heard his key turn the lock. I gave him a second to take in the scene and then I stepped out the bathroom.

I found him in his office sitting on the edge of the bed.

As seductively as I could, I walked over to him and began to remove the short robe that barely covered my ass.

I was trying to read the expression on his face, hoping I would find some form of delight in his eyes. The next thing I knew his phone was ringing and he had his hand in my face sshhh-ing me!

What the fuck?

There I was damn near naked, oiled up and ready to get freaky with my husband and he was pushing me to the side!

There were men who would pay a small ransom to be able to caress a body as beautiful as mine and my own husband couldn't care less!

All the time and effort I had put into this evening.

How was I supposed to hold onto this? He didn't even have the decency to tell the 'caller' he was busy!

Sean pushed me aside and walked right past me, leaving me standing there looking foolish and alone.

Who the fuck was he talking to that he had to take the call in another room, and leave me standing here like this? What could be that important!

I was so pissed and hurt, I felt invisible.

After 10 minutes of me just standing there in complete shock, I walked up to the bedroom where he was.

"Where are my boys?" He asked when I walked in the room, not even looking up at me.

"I sent the kids with Dawn for the night, so we could spend some time together Sean." I may have sounded a bit whinier than I intended, I knew that pissed him off, but I was pissed too!

"We are together every day Mariah", his tone, so dismissive.

I tried to hold it together, but he didn't even so much as mention a single thing about me, my attire, the roses, the music, nothing!

I walked over and stood directly in front of him, hoping my thick thighs would grab his attention....they didn't.

"Baby I went out of my way to prepare a nice quiet seductive evening for you and I."

"Listen Mariah, I am sorry you went out of your way, with all of....this," he looked like he had a nasty taste in his mouth, "but I am tired." he dryly stated as if he was watching paint dry on a wall.

I went over and stood in front of the mirror. I couldn't understand, anyone with eyes would consider me a very pretty woman, and my body was not bad, actually I looked damn good, even if this fool didn't appreciate it!

I had had enough!

"So you come home to your wife in lingerie, drinking, waiting to be fucked by YOU; HER HUSBAND and you don't even look at me!?! Are you gay, are you fucking someone else, what the fuck Sean!?"

"Here you go again Mariah. What is it that I am not doing for you? What have I failed to provide? You have a life you could have only dreamed of and yet you constantly find something to be upset over! Dawn would love to be in your place, maybe you should take some of her advice."

"WHAT?" He knew mentioning another woman would piss me off but I wasn't going to let him create a diversion and get me off topic, I needed to know why he had no interest in me any longer.

I wanted to punch him in his face! He had never been introduced to that side of me and I left her back in the projects with the rest of my family for this life, but now I was wondering if that was the best choice.

"You ruin the mood Mariah, all your complaints."

"How did I ruin the mood? I set the fucking mood Sean!"

"Watch your mouth Mariah; you are not in the projects!"

"I don't have to watch anything, I am an adult! You need to stop trying to chastise me and learn how to talk to me!"

"I don't have anything to say, I'm tired, I tried to tell you that, but you won't listen!"

I hated when he did this, he made everything my fault, twisted all my words and made me feel like shit! There was a time when we were out at a restaurant and we had a few drinks and were both feeling tipsy and frisky, or at least I was.

I asked him if we could climb in the back seat of his Mercedes and have some fun on our way home and somehow that conversation turned into an argument!

I was so tired of him making ME feel crazy, and shit, if I was, it was him that drove me to it!

"Fuck you!"

I was pissed and he was gonna hear my two cents either way. I had nothing to lose.

"You know I don't know a man in America that wouldn't want to come home to this! I mean I have candles, roses, chocolate, music, vodka, and somehow I KILLED THE MOOD? I am a woman Sean and I want to be made to feel like one, by my husband. It is not fair that I have to beg to be touched by you! You don't care how you make me feel or how I feel period! It is like you lack emotion and you are a complete rock to my affection! I don't even know how we made two babies!"

I didn't care if I had gone too far, I spent too many years silenced, he needed to know that I was one step away from an affair.

Without the slightest bit of emotion he replied, "I never said I didn't want to have sex with you, I said I was tired. Now I am saying I don't want to have sex with you. Excuse me."

He walked past me and went into the bathroom to take his shower, the shower I planned to take with him.

What a fucking Jerk!

I had exhausted all options and after the way he made me feel I was completely devastated as a woman and as a wife.

What did I do wrong?

I was unable to get through to him no matter what I tried. I was a piece of property to Sean, a toy. He would play with me when he wanted to, which was far too far in between. This is what I had to deal with in exchange for this life everyone else seemed to love so much.

I felt the tears running down my cheeks before I even knew I was crying. I was so tired of not being heard in this marriage.

What man refuses to please his woman? I thought to myself as I headed to the kitchen in search of my vodka. I had a platter of fruit and cheeses along with 2 glasses of wine and 2 shot glasses for the liquor.

"Fuck it!" I said as I tipped the bottle to my mouth, this was clearly a party for one, no need for glasses.

I was done crying, done feeling sorry for myself, done being a victim of these circumstances.

If I could just get him to listen, I know he would understand, but the problem was I never got the time of day with him.

I decided to text him although he was only a matter of yards away from me, because when we talked, it always leads to arguing so maybe this way he would hear me out as he read my words.

TO: Sean my Love 8:13pm

Daddy, I don't know where we go wrong every single time. I never set out to offend you, but it seems as if I am always making you upset. I am not happy sexually Sean and I haven't been for a while. I know you are able to please me and make me feel like a woman should, but it seems sometimes as if you don't want to. It's like we go into this routine and everything is so boring. There is no foreplay, no kissing; no caressing just basic sex. I should be able to tell you this, and it is your job as my husband to try and fix this. We can fix this Sean! We are married, this is how it goes! If we have an issue, we discuss it and then we work towards the resolution. As your wife I do my part Sean, because I do not want another woman to have something I lack and take your attention away from me. I have tried to be all that you desire, but I don't even know what that is anymore, but I don't think it's me. I yearn for certain feeling from you, I find myself fantasizing about all of the

47

**things that I don't get at home
so much it makes me afraid
Sean. I don't want to think
about another man. Why
would you leave me
unsatisfied? Are you not
afraid of what may be out
there to tempt me? Have you
ever thought how hard it
would be to turn down water,
when you're dying of thirst?**

I know I was going in on the text but he needed to
know all that I had been feeling, he needed to know
what this was doing to me.

I know for a fact that I loved my husband, he is a great
father and a wonderful provider. He is a hard worker
and came home every evening at a respectable hour.
We just didn't seem to connect on an intimate level
and I couldn't figure out why. I did not want to lose
my marriage, but i didn't know how much longer i
could stay. I did not want to be with another man, but
Sean was leaving me no options. I wanted this mess to
end so we could fix this problem he seemed to be
content on ignoring.

I looked at the message on my screen and
contemplated hitting send. Was I really going to tell
my husband that I was yearning to be with someone
else, because he wasn't satisfying me? I decided yes,
not to offend him, but in hopes to fix the issue in our
bedroom.

-send

I held my breath.......two minutes later.....

**FROM; Sean my Love 8:17pm
Goodnight Mariah.**

****

I must've cried myself to sleep that night because the next thing I remember was hearing Sean in the bathroom upstairs getting ready to go in to the office. Unless he took the boys to see his mom he always went to work for a few hours on Saturdays to catch up and prepare for the following week.

I hurried to the kitchen to make him some coffee and prepare his lunch. I was a robot with my household duties, come rain or shine, I did my part.

He came down sooner than I had anticipated as I was spreading a thin layer of mayo on a slice of wheat bread for his sandwich.

He walked straight past me, no good morning, no nothing and headed towards the door.

"Hey, I am almost finished with your lunch; I have your coffee all set." I said pointing to his mug on the counter.

"I will see what's out there to tempt my appetite today, no thank you."

He walked out the door and if I am not mistaken slammed it on his way out, so much for trying to face the problem head on.

I guess this is how he would show me he didn't like my text last night.

He played the victim so well.

I was nearing the end of my rope. Any judge would grant me alimony and child support. I was trying to convince myself I would be ok if I left Sean. Maybe it was time for me to throw in the towel.

I watched him back out the driveway and drive down the street.

The plan was to rock his world all night long and then top the morning off with a quickie right on the counter before he went out the door. He'd spend all day reminiscing on how I rocked his world and he'd hurry home for another round.

My thoughts drifted to the tall man who paid for my water the other day, I had forgotten his name but I couldn't get the face out of my head, and his smell and those damn dimples.

Chapter 5

I sent Dawn a text asking her if she wanted me to pick up the boys and take them to school. She quickly responded, no and suggested that I enjoy life's sweetest hang over.

I didn't dare tell her about my horrible night.

I knew better than to tell another female the troubles I had with my man, friend or not and I certainly wasn't going to embarrass myself any further reliving last night's events. I was already devastated enough.

I poured myself a shot of vodka; it was going to be a long miserable day.

After mellowing in my misery I decided to get off the couch and at least take the car to get looked at so I could say I did something productive today if I had to give Sean a report of my whereabouts for the day.

I hadn't realized how late it was nor did I realize that I had no idea where to take my car to. Since I assumed it was the brakes, I drove down a street in a commercial area looking for any shop with the word brakes on their sign.

As fate would have it, I found something in the same plaza I had walked to a few weeks ago, not too far from my house.

I figured I would stop since it was right there, and even if this wasn't the right type of mechanic I would convince him to ride around the block with me to help diagnose my ride and maybe point me in the right direction.

When I got up to the door it was locked, I peered to see inside by cupping my hands against my face on the glass, no one was inside as far as I could see

"Can I help you Ms.?"

I turned around and forgot everything I wanted to say.

It was him.

I didn't remember his name but I'd never forget that face and when he realized who I was he smiled and that dimple appeared.

God this man was fine.

"I ummm, I am having an issue with my car that um, I am not really sure about, but I think the brakes may....." I was rambling.

"Don't stress yourself beautiful, let me have the keys."

I liked when he called me beautiful. I was having a hard time looking away.

"Riri"

"Hunh, yes?" I liked that he called me Riri too.

"The keys Beautiful."

"Oh," I had to damn near die before Sean would even drive in the car to help me try to diagnose the issue and this stranger knew to take over immediately and assist me with solving my problem. He was already making my life easier.

I passed him the keys and hopped in the passenger seat.

"I love a girl who keeps a clean car"

I just laughed realizing how nervous I was. I hadn't been around another man alone in this close proximity in a long long time.

"Thank you, I...."

"Sshhhhh!" He shushed me and then rolled down the window, he was working, trying to figure out my vehicular dilemma.

"Riri, your brakes are horrible! You didn't see this brake light on?"

I leaned over to see the brake indicator and found myself a little closer than I should have and that sweet sensual masculine aroma invaded my nasal passageway, I was under a spell. I was so deprived at home, here I was sniffing this funky man, like a dog in heat and loving it!

"I hadn't noticed that. "

"I thought you told me you were married."

"I am!" I replied instantly.

"Well does your 'husband' ever drive this car?"

"No"

"Did you ask him to look at it?"

"My husband doesn't get his hands dirty he isn't a mechanic he is an executive." I regretted that statement as soon as I said it.

"Real men don't cry about a little dirt Ma, so he doesn't take care of the car, he obviously doesn't take very good care of his lady either. You could have crashed and been seriously hurt!"

I didn't like the way he way eyeballing me.

"Look I'm sorry, umm, uh, I forgot your name" I admitted slightly embarrassed.

"Rell"

"Right Rell, maybe now that we have identified the issue you can recommend somewhere I can take my car to be serviced" I was starting to feel uncomfortable.

"I can take care of this for you, it'll take me 20 minutes, on the house too. You can consider me your guardian angel, since I am literally saving your life right now."

I felt like shit hearing how dangerous the situation was. I was going to take it out on Sean as soon as he got home. Monday was always a late night for him, sometimes he would be in the office until Midnight, but he would certainly hear about this!

We got back to the shop and he let me out in front and then drove my car around back and inside the shop, he then came and opened the door for me.

He told me to make myself confortable, gave me bottled water and then ignored me and went right to work on my car. I was grateful he had the right sized brakes in his stock.

I didn't realize that my boys had been out of school until Dawn texted me, I had totally lost track of time.

> **FROM: Dawn 3:45pm**
>> **I came by to drop the boys off and neither cars were there, I have leftovers at home so I can just keep the boys with me, we are going to go to my house and have dinner for now, if I don't hear from you I will have them get ready for bed by 8. Love you.**

Dawn was such a good friend; I truly loved her and hoped someday she found a man to give her the world.

> **TO: Dawn 3:49pm**
> **KK**

Rell had removed his shirt and was now working in a dingy white wife beater. His body was that of a Greek god and African warrior mixed together.

There was something so attractive about this man and the way he knew just how to take control, come in and save the day.

I uncrossed and re-crossing my legs, trying to ignore the tingling going on between my succulent thighs.

He kept catching me looking at him

The third time I held my gaze as did he and we just starred at each other.

He smiled, flashed that dimple and continued to work putting his head down.

What the hell was I doing?

My kids were with a sitter, my husband working late and I in this mechanics office eye fucking his employee.

"Come here Riri"

"uh-ok"

I stood and straightened my clothes and walked into the room where he had my car lifted in the air.

"Yes?" I said softly.

"Why you keep looking at me Ms. I have a husband?" He didn't even look up he just keep working. I was thankful he didn't, my face must have been so red.

"uh......." I truly didn't know what to say, I was caught off guard.

"Do I make you nervous?" he said, head down still working.

"No."

"So talk to me" he seemed to be trying to lighten the mood, "do you have kids?"

I opened up to him after he asked me about my kids and like any other proud mother of course I had a million stories to tell who ever would listen about my 2 amazing little men.

Once he had my guard down, he reproached his target.

"If you were my lady you wouldn't be here, I would have taken care of this for you."

My guard may have been coming down, but I wasn't about to discuss Sean with this man or any other man, so I remained silent.

"Well', he said, "it seems like you have it all, but I can tell from the stress in your face that you're not being treated right. You get nervous and awkward at the simplest things; I can tell you're not used to receiving certain treatment. You know, things your rich husband can't buy in stores. Now don't jump down my throat I can see you are used to the finer things. Shit the only reason my shop is here is because yall rich folks can be over charged for everything and not even notice. I could never charge these prices in the hood. Certain women 'take' more comfortably than they should, but you are uncomfortable taking, even if it is something as simple as water."

He was killing me softly and there was nothing I could say. He must have taken my silence as permission to proceed.

"There is something else I can see too, it's written all over your face; your man's money don't satisfy you and neither does he. Don't cheat yo'self treat yo'self beautiful. I could be your emergency dick in a glass, no disrespect just saying I have the solution to your problem."

He stood up and lowered my Jag to the ground.

"No charge love, I'll meet you in the front."

He walked off leaving me standing there with wet panties.

I snapped out of it and headed out the front door to get my car.

"What would your boss say to you for doing this for free? At least let me pay you." I insisted trying to gain control of this situation.

"I own the joint Riri, you overlook too much, that may be dangerous, something could be right in front of you......you gotta be sharp."

I was about to roll my neck and show him my other side, telling me what I ought to do, when I looked up and not only seen his name but also his face on the sign. He must've thought I was a complete airhead.

We both laughed.

"Thanks Rell."

"No problem Riri, can I get a hug?"

I hesitated, looking his frame up and down, my panties were already soaked.

Shit, I had already slept with him in my head anyways so I gave in and hugged him.

He moaned a low growl in my ear as he held me close. I allowed him to keep me in his arms and I didn't try to fight.

"Does he not hold you like this?" Rell asked, while still holding me.

"No." I whispered.

He let go first. I was lost in the moment; I hadn't hugged my husband with such a warm embrace in what felt like forever.

Rell backed up and took me by my shoulders looking in my eyes.

"Riri, if you need me I am here ok?"

"Thank you Rell." I took my keys and walked off not bothering to look back.

I felt so pathetic, the fucking greasy mechanic at the corner store could probably love me better than my own fucking husband, but yet I stayed.

I drove home feeling depressed.....and horny.

Dawn had called to tell me not to worry about picking up the kids, we were on the phone when I heard a strange noise.

ting....ting....ting....ting...

What the hell was that? I said.

ting....ting...ting....ting...

"What was what?"

"Nothing girl, I will be there in the morning to take the boys to school, I gotta go."

ting....ting....ting...

Was that a phone? I bent down to the floor while still trying to look over the steering wheel at traffic. I retrieved the phone from the floor beneath my feet.

ting....ting....ting...

Whoever it was did not plan on giving up, I had to answer or it was driving me crazy.

ting...ting...ting...

What a stupid ring tone, I thought.

"Hello," I said in a shaky voice.

"Hello?"

"Yes?"

"Is this my phone?"

"It isn't mine, who is this please?"

"This Rell."

My heart skipped a beat. I was so caught up in feeling sorry for myself I had forgotten all about Rell just that fast.

15 minutes later I was walking up to a hotel on the north side of town.

I stood in the elevator so long after it reached his floor that the doors closed twice.

Slowly I stepped off of the elevator. I walked down to room 112, knocked twice and stepped back.

I could not believe that I was here, at a hotel, to drop off a phone.

I knew damn well what I was doing, and something told me Rell did too.

He opened the door and his sweet scent slapped me in my face.

"Hey. I just came to return your phone, so, here's your phone." *Really Mariah?* I was such a lame.

"That's all you came to give me?"

"Excuse me?"

"You heard what I said."

We had a stare down, neither of us able to look away.

He knew what he wanted; he just needed the green light from me.

Was I ready for this?

Sensing my apprehension, he pulled me into his embrace. I allowed myself to let go in his arms.

He leaned down and put his lips on mine, and I allowed that too.

I don't know what came over me but I decided to let go and give in. I may not have been around another man in a while, but there wasn't much new about them and I knew when a man wanted me. Rell and that sexy ass dimple wanted me from the evening we met.

I needed this and tonight I was going to get it.

I would fuck him and then never see him again.

I ripped his shirt off; he had clearly showered because he had on a crisp white wife beater and smelled like the heavens.

I stood back and admired his shirtless body. I bit my lower lip as I kicked off my shoes. I tugged at my jeans to get them below my hips and wiggled them the rest of the way down jiggling my titties the entire time. I unhooked my bra and stepped out of my panties too.

My nakedness must have given him all the assurance that he needed because he immediately began to devour my body. He buried his face into my neck and tried to kiss me, but I did not want to kiss him, I wanted to fuck him, so I told him.

"Rell" I moaned, "Don't kiss me and don't make love to me I want you to fuck me. Do you understand?

"I don't need a coach Riri and I know exactly what you need. I got this." He looked over my body with hunger in his eyes.

I took his hand and used it to play with my pussy. He felt so good.

Just as the sensation was building up I removed his hand and inserted two of his fingers into my mouth, and then in his.

"Damn Riri!" He sounded weak like he was begging that I give him more...

He pushed me down on the bed, and put his face in my neck again, planting soft kisses.

I pushed his head down to my nipples.

He latched on and began to sucking immediately.

"Bite me" I demanded.

He bit my nipple gently.

"Harder!"

He bit it harder.

"Harder!" I yelled.

He looked at me for a second and then followed my command.

"Ohhhhhhhh!" I moaned. God, it felt so good, his mouth was so warm.

I could tell it was turning him on too cause he was moaning, Sean never made a peep. He began nibbling on my nipple as I screamed his name and came all over his sheets.

When I opened my eyes he was just staring at me.

I didn't feel uncomfortable either, I stared back.

"Oh I see what you need Ma." Rell said just above a whisper.

"Mmmmmmm, let's see what else is down here that hasn't been touched in a while...."

Rell left a sloppy wet trail all over my breasts and down my stomach to my love below.

I like it nasty and he was turning me on so much.

He buried his face in my pussy and sniffed me like fresh laundry.

'Mmmmmmm" he growled again.

"Can I bite this too?" He looked at me with pleading eyes.

"You can do whatever you want."

He ate me like a peach dragging his teeth along my pussy lips, the feeling was so intense.

I had never, ever, had a man bite and chew on my pussy, sweet baby Jesus I came three more times and he still hadn't even penetrated me yet.

We changed positions, he wanted me to sit on his chest and ride his face. I couldn't believe he let me do it, actually he begged me to do it, begged me to grind harder!

I had never had oral sex like that in my life.

He laid me on my back and held my legs up and sucked my pussy dry.

I tapped out when he had me stand over him as he tried to cover every inch of my pussy with his mouth. My knees couldn't hold up any longer and I begged him to stop.

He refused and made me cum so hard I watched it drip into his mouth. He was so nasty and so was I! This was just what I had been missing.

When he stood up my legs automatically fell over his shoulders with my pussy still in his face.
He gently blew on my clit and just like that, I was ready for more!

He laid me on the bed, on my stomach and instructed me to arch my ass. Once I was positioned appropriately he got behind me.

I closed my eyes, anticipating the feeling of his entry, but it never happened.

Instead I felt a tickling sensation at the curve of my back; it was his tongue, ever so gently sliding down the crack of my ass, leaving a sloppy trail behind. I almost lost my balance and fell flat on the bed, but he held me up. He put his other arm around my stomach to help me hold my arch; he then proceeded to devour my pussy from behind.

Using both hands he spread my ass and dove in, smothering himself between my cheeks. He would plunge his tongue in and out of both my holes, bringing me to complete ecstasy.

"Want me to make that pussy cum over and over? Is that what you want Baby? Hunh? You need someone to take care of this pussy for you?"

I was unable to respond, multiple orgasms had me at a loss for words. Rell wasn't looking for confirmation, like he had said earlier; he knew exactly what I needed.

"I'm gonna cum Rell……….Re……Rell, oh God….mmmmm!"

"Yeah, cum for me! Put it on my face!"

This man was a freak and I loved every minute of it!

I smeared my loving all over his face, as requested.

"Yeah, mmmm, yeah, there is it."

It was hard to understand what he was saying because he literally devoured every ounce of my love juice. He sucked and slurped every drop.

"Can I bite your ass?"

"What?"

"Can I bite it Baby?"

My request from earlier must have turned him on and now he wanted to bite me all over.

"Come here" I purred.

I was trying my hardest to look back at him, I was on my knees doggy style but I wanted to see his face buried in my ass, I had waited a long time for this feeling, I needed a visual logged into my memory bank.

When his face was close enough to mine, I kissed his mouth, before letting go I sucked his bottom lip, savoring the flavor.

"I told you, you can do whatever you'd like." I whispered in his ear.

Rell went into overdrive and pleased me orally from every angle possible.

Even after I tried to tap out, he made me cum one last time.

He felt like heaven. I couldn't tell if I was standing right side up or upside down.

My body was exhausted and I didn't know what to say or do next. I felt like I owed him something…

"Rell…..I think…"

"You don't owe me anything Ma that was on the house. I wanted to taste that pussy since I first laid eyes on you. I am a man right, and you're a woman, not my woman but a woman none the less, it is a man's job to take care of woman, this is the easy part. Pleasing you is effortless. I'm not gon speak on your ol' boy, and neither should you, just know I know what you need and so does he. The difference is I will make you happy and keep you satisfied. Don't worry why he won't, you don't need him for that anymore. I can fill that void for you. You needed that." He laughed and shook his head.

I wondered what he was thinking.

"….and before you start feeling bad and having second thoughts, like you women do, we didn't have sex, no penetration, so technically you didn't cheat. I don't know if you're ready for all that yet anyways, and the last thing I want to do is scare you off." He kissed my lips and went into the bathroom.

I liked Rell, no pressure and lots of pleasure. He made me feel so good and so comfortable. Unfortunately I needed to get home, so off of cloud nine I had to come.

I went into the bathroom after he came out and got myself together.

I took his number kissed his cheek and left.

Chapter 6

I woke up in good spirits, it was Sunday, our family day and I would see to it that we would have a good one.

Sundays usually ended in sex, it just seemed the appropriate way to end off our day. The last thing I wanted to do was start it off bad and ruin my chances of a happy ending.

I heard Sean and the boys downstairs having cereal, the appetizer to my famous cinnamon French-toast.

I made the bed and threw on a pair of sweat pants. I almost put on a pair of legging but I thought against it. Sean despised leggings, said they were 'rachet' (why did I ever teach him that word), but I'd be damned, cause when we were together, I'd catch his staring at every single pair of ass cheeks that jiggled past us in those same leggings, bastard.

I decided to get into the bathroom before I pissed myself off, I vowed to stay optimistic. I brushed my teeth, threw my hair in a messy bun and hurried downstairs to cater to my men.

"Hi Mommy!"

"Hi poppa!" My baby Sammy, he was still very much in love with his mother and being my baby, although his father hated it.

He reached out to give me a hug.

"My wittle man is so sweet." I kissed all over his face as he giggled.

"He is being a gentlemen Mom, boys aren't sweet daddy said."

"Like this," Sean Jr. grabbed my hand and kissed it.

"Chivalry is indeed well and alive in this house! Your father is grooming the perfect gentlemen hunh?"

"My thoughts exactly!' Jr. replied. That boy was too much and too damn smart, I shook my head smiling.

"Morning Daddy" I pecked my husband on the cheek.

"Eeewwwww" Baby Sammy yelled causing us all to laugh.

"That is her husband, boy! How do you think you got here?" Sean Jr. asked.

"No I didn't! I came from heaven. I was a gift from God mommy said it!"

"Actually..." SJ had stood up prepared to school his little brother on where babies come from.

"SJ!!" I couldn't control my laughter but I had to cut him off.

"Dad, you said..." this kid was on a roll.

I had to get started with breakfast; I walked off laughing as I gathered my secret ingredients.

I overheard Sean telling SJ that Sammy was too little to be told 'everything', he said Sammy was still a cub, but he was a young lion, which is why he knew more than his little brother. SJ loved the idea of the hierarchy and that his position was above his Sammy's, so he'd keep their secret until the time was right.

"Your right Dad" I heard SJ tell his father.

I loved moments like these; I wouldn't trade them in for the world.

My thoughts shifted to Rell, and what we had done. I hadn't seen him since, 'that day'.

For so long I had to fantasize about passion and attention, it felt good to have received that from someone. My heart hurt that it couldn't be Sean, but my mind refused to let me feel bad. My body had been satisfied and I would make no apology for that.

I got so pissed sometimes that I had to go through all these emotions when Sean moved about as if life was perfect!

Why couldn't he see how close we were to true happiness? Why couldn't he see that I was hanging on to the edge of the cliff, barely holding on, desperately pleading with him to save me, to save us?

We had it all, almost.

There was no way Sean didn't know he was cold towards me, why was the question.

I felt the tears begin to swell....

I would change my appearance, keep my body in shape, I kept his home together and his boys educated and reared properly. What more could I do?

As soon as the first tear threatened to fall I knew I had to grab a hold of myself. My breakdowns were reserved for when Sean wasn't home. He was completely unable to deal with emotion.

I cried so much, so many tears of frustration over the years. There was something about being so close that makes the failure that much harder to deal with.

"God, what's wrong with you now?" Sean startled me, I didn't even know he was behind me, his tone was an annoyed one.

"Nothing" I quickly wiped the one tear that had escaped.

"Then why are you just standing over the stove like you have a problem?"

"Nope, I had something in my eye and I was trying to blink it away but I think I got it. What you need Daddy, something to drink?"

I tried to quickly change the subject.

It was little things, just like this, that could start a war in my home and we wouldn't speak for two and three days after. I refused, not today.

I grabbed his empty cup from his hand, rinsed it and had him a fresh glass of juice, ice and all before he could say another word.

"Now get out my way so I can cook, and stop trying to see my secret ingredients."

He just looked at me and walked out. I wasn't sure if he was convinced or not but at least it went no further.

We made it through breakfast without incident. We all played board games after I cleaned the kitchen.

That afternoon, Sean took the boys out in the yard to throw the ball around while I prepared a lite lunch and started on dinner.

After dinner later that evening we had ice cream sundaes and watched 2 movies.

The boys were out for the count, but I still had to fight to get them both into bed.

I rushed to the shower in a hurry to climb in the bed next to my husband.

He was asleep.

Unless he was upset at me Sunday nights were our nights. Sean would take a quick shower while I got the boys situated and then he'd wait for me, but not tonight.

I thought about what it would take to get him up and decided I'd be better off pleasing myself. I had a drawer full of toys, and a mind full of memories.

If he only knew that another man had touched me. The way he touched me, the way he kissed me. He caressed my body in all the ways my husband should have. He licked and sucked and controlled my body, giving me a preview of what it would be like to go all the way with him. I knew if I saw him again, there would be no way I wouldn't give him all of me, especially since I had no one else to give myself to.

I huffed and puffed before moving to the far side of the bed.

How long was I supposed to endure this? What man denied his wife?

I didn't need much, shit I had everything money could buy, every sex toy my money could buy.

I wanted to make love, to ride him, let him bang it from the back, he could put it where ever he wanted, I'd do whatever he said, and I could do it all with a guilt free conscious because he was my fucking husband!

God created woman for man, there was nothing better in this world than the closeness you feel during passionate love making; truly heaven on earth. A pleasure no married woman should be denied.

I was going to snap and loose it!

I wanted sex, or maybe I needed sex, no I yearned for it.

Our marriage was in the danger zone.

The itch was growing uncontrollable......

I had already begun rubbing my itch; I was trying as hard as I could not to scratch.

I laid in that bed, right beside my husband and began touching myself. I licked my fingers saturating them with saliva and began rubbing my clit, while the other hand massaged my c-cup sized breast. I pinched my nipple, remembering the way Rell made me feel. I parted the two lips of my love below and inserted a finger into my warmth, imagining it was Rell's tongue.

God, he made me feel so good.

Careful not to moan I continued to please myself, winding my hips in a circular motion. I removed my finger and put it in my mouth, I remember taking Rell's fingers from inside me and tasting them, that drove him crazy.

I wanted to imagine that he was here and pleasing me like I knew he could. Thoughts of him intensified the situation inside of me that threatened to overflow, I was gonna cum.

My waterfall drizzled all over the bed on the same sheets I shared with my husband.

Satisfied I drifted off to sleep with the thoughts of another man in my head as my husband slept by my side.

Chapter 7

I hadn't given Sean any attitude, nor did I make any attempts to have sex with him, and neither did he with me.

Rell and I had been texting each other daily. He was so sweet.

It was Friday night. Sean and the boys were asleep. They were going to spend the following day with his mother, a trip in which I was not invited.

I couldn't have cared less about not being invited! I would have declined anyways; I had my own plans and was glad I wouldn't have to make up a lie to get out of the house.

Had I have not had those plans though, I would have been pissed.

For one thing, why was I not invited?

Those were my damn kids, I delivered them into this world yet I was always excluded. Two, Sean has never taken a Saturday off to spend some time with me, but once a month he could to spend the day with his mom! He always told me he had to work, and made sure to remind me that he was the only earner in the home, making me feel like shit. I certainly couldn't argue with him and that is just the way he liked me, quiet! I wanted to say that it was his idea that I was a stay at home mom, but I never said anything.

I usually would give Sean a piece of my mind about my exclusion yet again, even though I would be ignored, but not that time. I packed their bags with urgency and damn near suggested that they leave that night!

I had a date planned with Rell tomorrow. Technically our first date, and I was excited.

Surprisingly I wasn't nervous at all about spending the day with him.

Sean paid me zero dollars in attention and would go all day outside of the house and never even call to check on me. Yes the boys were with him when he would do that but what about me?

I was confident I wouldn't be missed due to his pattern of negligence and I couldn't wait to be next to Rell again, maybe we could even finish what we started.

After getting the boys all packed for their day trip to their Granny's house I went to bed, in a rush to get to the next day.

****

When I awoke the house was empty.

That bastard couldn't send the boys in to kiss me goodbye.

My thoughts went immediately to Rell; I grabbed my phone to see if he had text. No luck, but I did get a text from Sean, one word; 'gone', as if I wouldn't be able to figure that out.

Just as I was about to put my phone down it vibrated in my hand, an instant smile appeared across my face.

> **FROM; Auto Repair 10:23am**
> **Good morning Riri. Are you awake?**

> **TO; Auto Repair 10:23am**
> **Yes**

> **FROM; Auto Repair 10:24am**
> **We still on for today, right?**

> **TO; Auto Repair 10:24am**
> **Yes**

> **FROM; Auto Repair 10:25am**
> **I will be in the food court parking lot waiting for you, can't wait to see you Riri.**

> **TO; Auto Repair 10:27am**
> **K. xoxo**

I hopped out of bed to get ready, 45 minutes later I was heading out the door in a Michael Kors maxi dress, Swarovski crystal encrusted thong sandals and lip gloss. I figured my attire would be appropriate no matter what we got ourselves into, plus I had packed a bag with a few other things in it, just in case.

When I pulled up to the mall parking lot, I realized I did not know what type of car he drove, forgetting that he knew mine, I text him.

TO; Auto Repair 12:03pm
I'm here

FROM; Auto Repair 12:03pm
I know, lol, come on.

I got out of the car and when I saw his face I instantly began to blush. My pussy jumped when I smelled his cologne. He was so sexy.

He walked up to me and gave me a nice tight, long hug. I loved hugs. I grabbed my bag from the trunk of my car, which he took away from me and put it in his trunk. He then opened my door for me to get in.

He drove a Jaguar 2 years newer than mine; it was all white and looked like creamy milk, *not bad for a mechanic*, I thought.

I wondered for a second if I should be concerned about his personal life, but I dismissed the thought as soon as it surfaced.

He hopped in the driver's seat, threw that baby in gear and let her rip. We were on the highway, heading to the neighboring city.

Rell understood my situation and only wanted to show me a good time, so we went out of town where we could do that in peace.

Just sitting in that passenger seat riding shot gun with him almost made me cry.

With Sean I felt so much anxiety whenever we went out. Although I had tried to communicate with Sean for years that I wasn't happy in our marriage, he completely and entirely ignored the situation.

He would take me out on holidays and the occasional date night but I was never happy. I would have to pretend that I enjoyed our quality time together, but I felt like a caged bird with him.

I could never laugh too loud, or be too polite without being accused of flirting.

If I displayed any sign of unhappiness he would escalate from 0-100 so fast, end the night, no matter where we were and he would bring me home, chastising and lecturing me the entire way.

With Rell I felt so free. I could breath.

I rolled down the window smiling to myself. The sun seemed to shine brighter.

"I don't care if we on the run........baby long as I'm next to you........"

I hummed along to Queen B who was blaring through the speakers as the wind blew in my face.

My soul was at such peace in that moment, and it was that same moment that I decided I was going to give myself to Rell.

I wanted more of him and the feeling he brought. I wanted to give myself to him.

"Rell?"

He turned down the music and signaled me to continue as he weaved in and out of traffic.
"Can we go back to that hotel?"

"Oh, you wanna go back to the Love nest?"

He briefly took his eyes off the road to read mine; he smiled knowing what I wanted, what I needed from him.

Without a word he turned the music back up, and placed his hand over mine. At the next opportunity he rerouted us to the love nest.

****

I stood by the bathroom, looking in the mirror.

What the hell am I doing? I asked myself. The last time I had on lingerie I made a complete fool of myself.

I had an entire drawer of sexy, sultry and slutty lingerie for my husband that I bought long before I realized the dynamics of my marriage.

I don't know what made me even pack it but I did and now I was wearing the lingerie I had picked out for my husband with another man. I stood in front of the mirror, second guessing myself.

Sean had really damaged my self-confidence.

I jumped when I felt Rell next to me. I was so lost in my thoughts that I hadn't even heard him come into the bathroom.

He didn't say a word. He just stood there and looked at me.

He looked at me, in a way my husband never had.

Somewhere between the bedroom and the bathroom he had lost his shirt and stood behind me.

I refused to feel sorry for myself; I was liberated and ready to seal the deal!

I looked into his eyes and then I had to look away. He was so intense, like he could see my soul.

"Can I have you?" He walked up so close to me I could feel the budge in his pants. He left a wet kiss on my shoulder.

Over my shoulder he stood as we locked eyes in the mirror.

My eyes said yes and he heard them loud and clear as he began to kiss my neck.

He kissed me like he was starving for my love.

"Mmmmmm" he moaned.

I wasn't really sure what to do. Sean didn't do foreplay and for the past 10 years he was the only man I'd been with.

Rell sensed my body tensing up; he grabbed my hand and wrapped it around his neck.

He smelled so good.

When he ran his hands over my breasts I arched my ass into him giving him the green light.

He took my hand and led me over to the bed. We stood face to face.

"Are you sure?" He asked, genuinely.

"Yes." I answered with confidence.

He bent down and kissed me in my mouth. Our tongues swapped spaces as they moved in sync like a choreographed dance.

He played with my ass, picking it up and dropping it, cupping it, squeezing it, slapping it and I loved every minute of it. His hands were like silk caressing my body. Sean always hinted about my weight and that my ass was getting bigger, Rell certainly didn't seem to mind this big ole' ass!

Next thing I know, he was picking me up, and I went with it and wrapped my legs around his waist.

He laid me on the bed and got on top, grinding his thick dick all over me, teasing me. He had me like a dog in heat and I wanted every inch of what was in his pants.

"Lay back" he instructed as he pushed me back on the bed.

I fell back and threw my legs on his shoulders like I knew he wanted me to.

And just like a cat licks up a bowl of milk, he licked my kitten, same sounds and all.

"Ooohhhh Daaaaaaaady" I moaned. I had my hands on his head, locking him in place.

He continued sucking as I held my legs up.

"Oh so you want me to get all up in it?"

"Yes" I purred like a kitten.

"You want Daddy to get in this pussy?" he spread both my pussy lips and stretched them apart.

I had no idea what would come next, but I was ready.

"Mmmmmm" he moaned starring at my pussy, he began talking to her, their own private conversation. "This pussy so pink Riri, so pretty, mmmm and it's even pinker inside. Ugghhhh. I wanna put my tongue inside you. Can I put my tongue inside you Riri? Hunh?"

"Yes Baby, put it inside this pussy, put it inside this pink pussy. Taste it baby, eat that pussy." I chanted.

He stiffened his tongue and penetrated me with it. His tongue pierced my pussy over and over and over. I must have cum in his mouth at least two times, but he didn't seem to mind at all.

The muscles in my legs locked up as I tightened my pussy around his tongue, coming for the third time.

"That's- right- cum- cum-for-me- I-wan t-you-to-cum-and-cum-and-cum." He said in between plunges.

Although his tongue could only reach so far, the sensation was bringing me so much pleasure.

He stood up to remove his pants; he was literally bursting at the seams.

I sat on the edge of the bed and ran my fingers through my hair.

I was so nervous, so many questions running through my mind.

Could I trust him?

Did I even know how to make love to a man like him? I could learn, and I am sure he'd teach me.

I looked over my shoulder and admired his physique.

He was so patient, as he quietly waited, giving me my moment.

I sat on the edge of the bed contemplating a moment longer. This was it, and I was ready. I slowly removed my wedding ring, sat it on the night stand……and then I removed my negligee.

I was as sober as a saint, I had no idea where this courage came from and I couldn't even blame it on the goose, this choice was all me.

"Can I trust you?"

"Riiiii, come here"

"Can I trust you?"

"Lay back" he instructed

I couldn't deny him or the way he made me feel.

My body was possessed and I was in heaven. So I laid back, just like he asked me to. I was going to enjoy every second of the sweet pleasure he provided.

I wanted this man to devour me; I wanted him so deep inside of me. I needed this.

My whole body was saturated with the sweat from our bodies. He knew just what to do and wanted every inch of my body to be under his spell.

"Rell" I lifted his head "Please, fuck me baby."

He took one last lick on my kitty, kissing her goodbye… although we both knew he'd be back.

He climbed on top of me. His sexy body glistening as he leaned down to kiss my face.

The sweet scent of my love was all over him.

I was so lost in his kiss, when he inserted himself inside of me I didn't even stop to think about a condom, it didn't matter cause it was already too late.

The feeling of his manhood penetrating my sweet spot was overwhelming. This was a whole new world I was exploring with this man, sharing with him, my most valued possession.

I was so wet, he entered me with ease.

"Damn Ri" He was also enjoying the new feeling inside of my sweet, sugary walls.

"Baaaaaby" I moaned, he was still making his entry and a grand entry it was.

I feel at least 10 inches of pure pleasure slowly making its way inside me. I could feel his pulse inside me as we lay motionless trying to savor that feeling that only happened the first time.

I closed my eyes and let my guard down.

I wanted him to feel as good as he was making me feel, so changed positions; I wanted to be on top.

I began slowly gliding my tight pussy up and down his rod. I contracted my muscles, giving him the ride of his life- his words, not mine.

"Oh shit, damn Ri, damn baby." He moaned, unable to keep his composure. "Wait Baby, you gonna make me cum, I don't wanna cu…."

"Sshhhh" I kissed his lips.

I had so much passion built up inside of me. "Cum Baby, I want you to cum, and I'll get it right back up" I moaned in his ear.

"FUCK Mariah!" he yelled. I had never heard him say full my name.

"Yes Baby?" I was in control bouncing my ass up and down on top of him all while keeping a nice grip on his pole. I grabbed his hands from my ass and put them on my breast.

He massaged and pinched my nipples causing pain and pleasure at the same time.

I was going to lose control!

I buried my face in his neck while still riding him. He grabbed my hips and slammed himself inside of me with urgency. I could tell he was going to cum….again, and so was I.

I released my muscles as my love poured all over him, he came with me.

We stayed in that very position, not moving for a few minutes longer.

I felt the sticky glaze of our lovemaking all over us. I didn't want it to dry and glue us together, so I tried to get up and get a towel, but he had other plans.

"Where are you going?"

"I was going to get you a towel, we are a mess." I laughed.

"Girl, get over here!" He held me in place. "For right now, this is my pussy and I like my pussy nice, wet, sticky and icky just like this. You smell so good."

I giggled.

"You feel that?" His dick was coming back to life inside of me. "You thought I was gonna let you get away with making me scream your name like that? Hold on" He smirked and wrapped his hand around my waist as he laid me on my back.

Our transition was a little awkward causing our bodies to separate. I felt his juices running down my thigh, I immediately felt embarrassed. Sean and I didn't have messy, sloppy sex, this was all new.

"What's wrong?" He noticed the change in my demeanor.
"Nothing" I didn't want to spoil the mood so I pulled him down on top of me kissing his lips. I reached down to insert him back inside of me. He was so thick and long.....God.

"I'm gonna make you cum again." He moaned, as he struggled to get both hands under my ass.
He used his grip to deepen his stroke, feeling him so big inside of me, so deep, the sheets were so wet, I thought we spilled a drink.

"Ooohhhh, I'm coming Baby, Oh, uuummmmm, I cominnnngggggggg" I whispered in his ear as he unleashed my fountain.

I had never had better sex in my life.

Rell pounded away, I loved that he loved to go so deep.

Sex with him was amazing and when I felt him insert his finger in my ass, I didn't stop him.

I wanted it all. He was making all my fantasies come true.

"Rrrreeeeellllllllll!" I couldn't help myself from crying out as his finger penetrated my asshole. "Yes Baby, yes." I whined the pain plus pleasure was euphoria.

"Uuuhhgggggg, cum with me Baby, lets cum together while I play in that ass," Rell moaned. "Look at me!" he demanded through gritted teeth.

I looked at him and then looked away, I couldn't.

"Look at me!" He pounded my pussy, my punishment for not complying. I pushed my hands against his chest to no avail as he continued to plunge his magic stick in and out my tight opening.

"Look at me Mariah." He demanded again, clearly this was a requirement so I locked eyes with him and tried my hardest not to look away.

I starred directly into his face as he fucked me and he starred into mine.

I wanted to tell him I loved him, but I didn't.

He was so intense and I was beginning to really think he wanted more from me than just my body.

Never had I been brought to such sexual heights.

A single tear fell from my eye as I came again, my creamy love moisture drenching the sheets.

He came too, for the third time….. inside of me.

He kissed my face.

He was so strong, yet gentle, so dominate yet considerate, the perfect blend.

"Turn on your stomach." he said.

I couldn't believe we were still going at it.

Lord where had this man been my entire life, I thought to myself as I turned over.

He took a second to admire the view before he reinserted that long, hard, dick.

I came right away.

"I can't get enough Baby." I panted out of breath.

He growled like a bear and began deep stroking my pussy from the back, the sound of our skin slapping echoing off the walls.

"Mmmm babyyyyy." I moaned, his deep stroke hurt so good.

"Lift up on your knees Ri." I followed his command. "Throw it back, yeah; put it on this dick baby"

On my knees, face down ass up I took him to heaven.

I bounced and clapped my ass all over him, matching every stroke.

My ass was bouncing so wildly he couldn't even keep his grip. I needed to repay him for all the pleasure he had given me.

He grabbed a handful of my hair, "Mariah, goddamn Ma, fuck. You want me to cum again? You want me to come inside this pussy Baby?"

"Yes….. please…. cum inside of me!" Tears were falling down my face, but I wasn't crying, this was ecstasy, an out of body experience.

He wrapped his other hand around my throat, and chocked me! Yes chocked me and I will be damned if that didn't magnify the feeling times a hundred!

My legs began to shake uncontrollably; I couldn't take it anymore collapsing on my stomach.

He had won and I damn sure didn't mind loosing.

I had read about being choked during sex. I believe it was called erotic asphyxiation.

I was against it, I thought it was dirty, degrading and something only whores did, to be honest, but truth be told, after experiencing it, I loved it! It was so intimate, exciting and sexy.
It was like I was his property to do with as he pleased. I'd always wanted to be controlled and dominated in the bedroom. It was my pleasure to be submissive, I didn't mind at all.

Our little walk on the wild side gave me the best orgasm of my life.

As a unit he rolled us on the side not missing a beat. He left this hand around my neck and used the other one to lift my thigh.

The wet gushy sounds of our love making turned me on so much.

This man was pulling my hair, chocking my neck and giving me the stroke of my life all at the same time!

I had long ago lost count but we came again, together.

"Mariah"

"Yes Baby"

"Damn girl"

"o-k," I laughed

"Hhhmmm" He moaned in my ear, snuggling up closer to me.

We stayed just like that. Neither of us moved or said a word. I wanted to get up and get him a towel but he still had his hand around my neck although his grip had loosened.

We must have fallen asleep because when I woke up my phone was going off and it was dark outside.

"Shit!" I said out loud in an instant panic. *What time was it? How did I let myself fall asleep?*

I had to pull and pry to get from underneath Rell who was still sound asleep.

My body was so sore.

I grabbed my phone, it was Dawn.

"Hello?" I whispered walking into the bathroom and locking the door.

"Where the hell are you? Girl why are you whispering? I came by the house earlier, you weren't there and I've been calling and texting you! Sean came by and…"

"Sean?! Sean was where? What was Sean doing at your house?" All of a sudden I felt sick.

He seemed to not be too fond of her, so what the hell was he doing at her house?

"He came by earlier on the way to his Mom's, Sammy left his blue hat, you know the one his Grandma got him, well he left it here and was having a fit so they stopped by and grabbed it. Are you sure you're ok?"

"Yes, I am sure. I have to go Dawn. I will call you back in a second."

"Hey wait, where are you? Sean called to see if I was with you because you weren't answering your phone."

How the fuck did Sean have her number?

I loved my friend but sometimes I just needed her to mind her business and stop trying to be an advocate for Sean all the damn time, she was supposed to be my friend and Sean didn't even like her, at least that is what he made me believe.

I didn't have time to figure that out now. I needed to get my ass in the shower and home before my husband got there or I would be in a world of trouble.

I would have to deal with Dawn later.

"I'll call you back D, gimme a sec."

I hung up before she could protest any further.

"Shit!"

I jumped in the shower and tried to wash the scent of our lovemaking off my skin.

There were marks all over my body.

Rell was rough, and although I had enjoyed it, I don't know what the hell I was thinking. We hadn't even used protection!

I had to get out of here.

I quietly put my clothes on and left without waking Rell.

I called a taxi to take me back to the mall to get my car. I tipped him a hundred dollars to get me there in lightning speed.

I pulled up to my house like a bat out of hell.

I cannot explain the relief I felt when I turned the corner and didn't see Sean's car.

Thank you Jesus! I prayed silently.

I ran upstairs, throwing my bag in the laundry room, some of those things needed to be cleaned and some needed to be burned, but I would handle that later. I placed the bag at the bottom of the laundry hamper & put the dirty laundry back on top.

I lived in a house full of men; no one came close to the laundry room besides me.

I hopped in the shower again; I needed to smell like 'myself' with my products instead of generic hotel soap.

I got in the bed, pretending to be asleep just as my men came in the door.

The boys must have been worn out because they usually would have come up the say goodnight to me but Sean sent them straight to bed, and for him they would go without a fight.

Ten minutes later he entered our bedroom.

"I called you. Then I had to call your friend looking for you, but apparently you weren't around for her either."

Now here I was, all the lights off, in bed, pretending to be sleep and he was having a regular conversation with me as if I was sitting up in the bed with the lights on.

I choose to ignore him, shit I was asleep! Even if I was faking it!

I was doing such a good job pretending to be asleep that I had actually started to doze off when my eyes jilted open in a panic!

Thank God my back was to him.

No, this couldn't be happening!

Nine point nine-nine-nine times I had to initiate sex, this would be the one time that he would actually want to have sex with me!

Sean was grinding on me from behind!

Sorry hun, I've actually been out getting fucked all day long while you and the boys were with your mom.

I felt like shit times ten!

I had to come up with something, *Think bitch think*, I said to myself.

In the fakest, phoniest voice I could muster I groggily said, "Hey Daddy, I didn't even know you and the boys were back. I have been in bed all afternoon; I am having the worst cramps ever. God! How was your Mom?" I sat up, yawned and then rubbed my stomach tried to lay it on as thick as possible.

I knew the word cramps would turn him off. He barely wanted to be next to me when I had my period, he was so grossed out by it.

"She is fine, and she said hi. Cramps hunh? Where were you all day? Dawn and I were trying to call you." He sounded suspicious.

"You know how hard I sleep. I took 3 pain pills and fell out; I've been sleeping all day."

"So you slept all day? Good then you won't be too tired to please your husband."

Great! That meant he wanted his dick sucked. I wouldn't mind but he had never in his life given me oral sex, yet he would ask me to do it for him! Ugh!

I sucked his dick for a whole three and a half minutes before he came in my mouth. It was so salty and tart not at all like the sweet love I had made earlier.

My thoughts drifted back to Rell……

"You gonna get me a wash cloth or what?" Sean barked, snapping me out of my daydream.

I was the one with semen all over my face, but he needed to clean me off of him!

As I cleaned Sean off, I compared him in every way to Rell.

Sean was so secure and dependable and stable. He was the father of my kids and my husband, but Rell had awakened something inside of me.

What had I gotten myself into?

Chapter 8

I hadn't spoken to Rell since we spent the day together last week. I had also been making sure to go to bed after Sean was already asleep so he wouldn't try to have sex with me.

I was Sean's birthday. The boys and I were making him a special dinner.

It wasn't that I didn't love my husband, because I did. It was just that there were certain things my husband wasn't giving me and hasn't given me for years and now that I had obtained such things I was happy.

"Mom, Mom.....Mom....MOM!" Sammy snapped me out of my trance, he was relentless, my little guy.

"Yes Baby?" I picked him up.

"I am not a baby! Please can you put me down?" he kicked his legs until they touched the ground.

"Alright, Momma's big boy, what can I help you with?"

"When, when, when, we were at Granny's house, Aunt D brought me my hat, she put it on my head and told me I was a cutie pie, but I don't want to be a pie Mom!" He screwed up his face.

My heart skipped a beat.

We were making a homemade apple pie from scratch, Sean's favorite, and I assume that is what triggered his little memory.

What is he talking about Dawn being at his Grandmother's house? I know goddamn well.....

"SEAN JR!" Sammy often times was confused about time and locations, he had just turned 5, but SJ was advanced and had the mind of a child twice his age.

"You called me Mom?"

"Do you remember a week or so ago when you, Sammy and Daddy went to your Grandmother's house?

"Yeeesss," He answered uncertainly.

"Who else was at your Grandmother's house?"

My first born son looked dead in my face and didn't say a word.

"Boy I know damn well you heard me! Now answer me!" I was beyond pissed and on the brink of losing control.

I didn't mean to yell and curse at my son, but I needed clarification on what Sammy had just said!

Sean Jr. was his father's child, and as stubborn as they come, he continued to stand there and defy me.

"Sean!"

He was nervous, but he held his ground. "My Father told me that I can't repeat what he does and to stay out of adult conversations."

I wanted to knock his head off his shoulders, but Sean did not play about the discipline of his boys and he believed that was his job. If I spanked him for being defiant and he told his father I would have hell to pay.

All hell was about to break loose anyway, but he was saved by the bell when I heard his father hit the alarm on his car in the driveway.

I walked off without another word, I needed to get myself together and figure out how I was going to handle this, because someone was going to give me some answers!

As I was heading back to the kitchen I heard Sean Jr. telling his Dad that I had questioned and yelled at him.

This little boy was telling on me!

Thirty-three hours, twenty-seven minutes and eighteen seconds of labor I went through to bring his little ass into this world and he went against me without a second thought!

Living in the house with three men, there was never any balance.

"You're not in any trouble son." Sean patted Jr. on the head and told him to go check on Sammy.

Why the fuck am I nervous, when he is the one who has some answering to do? I asked myself.

"I've told you this before, and I am going to tell you this again, Mariah, do-not-question-my-sons." He came in roaring.

The nerve of this mutha-fucker!

I wanted to tell him that I didn't question MY sons, and that Sammy had told because he's five and can't keep a secret to save his life, but I didn't want to get Sammy in trouble.

One would have never known that less than ten days prior I was getting dug-out by another man.
I was no saint but I knew enough to go outside, way outside of our circle of friends and associates.

If he and Dawn were creeping around behind my back I was going to kill both of them!

"Dawn told me you stopped by her house. I didn't even know you knew where she lived, let alone her number. Anytime I've told you she was coming over here you give me a look that says you wished she wasn't and you're always rude to her when she is around. I'm wondering, and pardon me for doing so but when did you two because such good friends!"

He looked at me like I had a third eye and just like his eldest son, said nothing.

If I didn't know any better I would think he enjoyed seeing me feel like this! I hated him!

"You would yell at me for letting her kiss the boys, even though it was just on their cheek and even though she is BOTH of their god-mother, but Sammy told me she was at your Moms kissing all over him. What the hell is going on Sean?"

Shit! I saw the expression change on his face when I said Sammy's name.

"So you were questioning both my boys? You look desperate and foolish and I am not going to entertain this conversation. You need to get a hold of yourself Mariah. I don't know what is wrong with you lately but you need to pull it together. Have you forgotten a few weeks ago when no-one could find you? Did I go around interrogating people? No!"

"Yeah, that's because you could care less about me!" I yelled, tasting the salt from tears that were streaming down my face.

His calm tone and demeanor was making me upset.

"Do you know what toady is Mariah? Today is MY birthday and all I wanted to do was come home and have a nice evening with my family, maybe even have sex with my wife, but no, you've ruined that for me like you ruin everything else. Thanks hun, you're the best!"

He walked away and left me to finish the conversation alone.

That was as violent as things got with Sean; he was very dismissive and knew just how to piss me off. Communication with this man was impossible; I don't even know why I tried.

Dawn had already told me that he was there, and Sammy does mistake time and locations, which we all knew as well. Why was I tripping? Dawn was my friend and would never do anything like that to me, but I didn't want to be the naive person who couldn't see what was right in front of them.

Was I tripping because I was cheating? Was I paranoid that everyone around me was as low down as I was?

I gotta get out of this house! I thought.

I didn't even tell him I was leaving. I grabbed my keys and made sure to slam the door on my way out!

I had no clue where I was going; I was just driving and thinking.

Dawn was my only ally.

Sean's Mom hated me, his sister despised me, he barely liked me and now he had turned my boys against me too!

110

I had to call her, but then I thought against it. I would look so crazy accusing her of betraying me.

Before I realized it I was driving down her street, pulling in front of her house. I wasn't going to interrogate her. I had nowhere else to go. She was truly my only friend.

I did not want her to be his friend. She was the only thing I had, that had not come from him and I needed her on my side.

How desperate was I to be ready to cry on the shoulder of a woman who may be trying to take my place with my husband?

I thought of all the times she had made comments about how she would love to have the things I had or how I should take care of Sean.

I sat there for about thirty minutes going back and forth, driving myself crazy when the vibration of my phone took me out my one sided debate.

> **FROM; Sean my Love 7:56pm**
> **Don't rush home, my boys & I**
> **are going out for ice cream.**
> **The apple pie burnt**.

Fucking asshole! Instead of trying to see what the problem was he would rather completely ignore me, which only infuriated me further.

I pulled off and headed home, at least I could shower and be in bed asleep before the boys returned and tomorrow would be a new day and hopefully bring a new outlook.

My phone vibrated again.

Say one more word and I am going off and I don't care!

I figured it was Sean, back to beat the dead horse. He loved to make me feel worst that I already did, and i was going to go in on his ass tonight!

> **FROM; Auto Repair 8:01pm**
> **Evening Beautiful. Can I see you tonight?**

It was Rell. My hearts skipped a beat but this time in a good way.

I wasn't really sure how I wanted to proceed with him, or even if I wanted to but right in this moment, I needed what he was selling.

I responded back:

> **TO; Auto Repair 8:02pm**
> **I'm actually out now, where are you?**

> **FROM; Auto Repair 8:02pm**

112

**…meet me at my shop, I'm
here now**

**TO; Auto Repair 8:03pm
omw...**

Without a second thought, I headed towards his shop.

I felt like I had no one, Sean had brainwashed the boys,
he was treating me like shit and my best friend was
possibly creeping with my husband! I needed Rell
right now.

I pulled up to his shop fifteen minutes later and drove
my car around the back.

He was standing outside on his phone, as soon as he
saw me, he told whoever it was that he'd have to call
them back. Sean always made me do the waiting.

"Something really important just came up Boss; I'll
have to call you back later on…..alright. Hey Riri." He
smiled flashing that dimple that I loved so much. He
walked up to me and hugged me so tight.

I found myself crying in his arms, and once I started, I
couldn't stop.

He didn't say anything, he just let me cry. He stood
there holding me in his strong muscular arms and let
me get it out.

In that moment I was so happy to have someone in my
corner, wrong or right, I silently thanked God for him.

At some point I stopped crying but had gotten so comfortable leaning into his chest that we were still standing there.

"Can I make you feel better?" He lifted by chin so he could look in my face.

I nodded my head yes.

I needed him. I needed to feel the way only he could make me feel.

He took my hand and led me into the shop. It was dark but he knew his way around and guided me effortlessly to our destination, which felt like a leather couch.

I didn't recall seeing a sofa the last time, but I was following his lead.

"Take your clothes off." He whispered, and I quickly complied.

Standing there in complete darkness and absolute nakedness I wasn't sure what he was doing.

I could feel his presence close to me but I wasn't sure if he was in front of me, on the side of me or what. I stretched my arms out trying to feel for him to no avail, but when I felt his warm tongue licking up the crack of my ass I knew he was behind me.

I turned around, interrupting his feast.

"Fuck me Daddy." I whined.

I didn't have time for his love making, we'd be all night! Today, I needed a nice quick fuck; I still wanted to beat Sean home.

"Say please." He saturated his fingertips with saliva and patted my pussy three times, she jumped from his touch.

"Please Daddy, please."

I prepared myself for his entry, a feeling I had been anticipating and fantasizing about since the last time.

He worked his way up to my neck; I didn't want to risk him leaving a mark of passion so I turned around.

"Oh so you really do want me to fuck you. I see....."

He grabbed a handful of my hair, turned me around so my back was once again facing him and pushed me forward, bending me over the sofa.

He used his other hand to guide his swelled dick inside of me.
"Daaaaaaddddyyyyyyy mmmmmmmm...." I had an instant orgasm.

"You cumming already?"

"Yessss, baby yes" I moaned.

"You said you want me to fuck you right?" He plunged himself so deep inside of me.

"Yyyeesss!"

"Tell me to fuck you then." He gripped my ass with both hand and spread my cheeks apart trying to go deeper.

"Fuck me Rell!"

"Mmmmmmm" He growled like a bear and fucked me like an animal. Wild and rough the entire time!

"I'm gonna cum again Rell, ooohhhhhh Babyyyy, uuggghhh"

"That's right, come all over this dick baby." I did just that.

Climaxing for a second time I felt our love-juice dripping down my inner thigh.

"Oooohhh yeah, I feel it, Daddy like that." He was still deep sea diving inside of me.

We went at it for another 10 minutes, in and out, deeper, harder, faster, so wet and gushy, the sounds our bodies made together, I drove him crazy!

"Goddamnnnnn Mariah! Shiiiittt....." He pulled out and spread his seeds all over my soft round ass.

After catching his breath, he went to turn the lights on, immediately I felt awkward standing in the middle of his shop naked with his semen dripping from my body.

Rell just stared at me.

I always caught him starring.

He looked at me like he wanted me to be his and that wasn't a topic for discussion, so I said nothing.

I think we both tried to deny that we were really falling for each other.

I gathered my jeans and thong from the floor and headed to the restroom to clean up and head home.

Chapter 9

For two weeks I was stuck in bed sick as a dog.

I was avoiding Rell at all costs, which wasn't hard, I simply blocked his number.

I needed a moment to think.

In those two weeks, I had really begun to re-think my actions, which were unfortunately too late to erase.

Rell had rocked my world in a way that I had longed for, but I had a life and a family. I had let my selfish desires jeopardize my entire family.

Rell was amazing, but only when it came to sex. We didn't have anything else, we didn't share anything else and we never discussed anything else.

I had two boys that he really didn't even know about.

I had jeopardized 80% to chase 20%. I was ashamed and depressed.

For the first couple of days Sean ignored me as usual, but the third day he came home to a chaotic house and no dinner he took notice.

Since then he had been attentive and concerned, which only made me feel even worst.

He was catering to me and I didn't even feel like I deserved his affection, even though that was the very thing I had been fighting for all this time.

I didn't want to kiss my children, I felt guilty thinking about all the things Rell and I had done and it made me feel filthy.

I even thought about all the unprotected sex we had. I was on birth control and taking them pretty regularly for the most part, so I wasn't concerned with an unplanned pregnancy, but what if I brought home something to my husband? I didn't know where this man had been! I had really fucked up.

I heard Sean on the phone with his mother, telling her that he was starting to get worried about me.

I wanted to disappear, my husband was finally starting to display husband like behavior but I no longer felt worthy.

How could I have done this to him, to our family?

How could I mold my sons to pursue descent woman when behind closed doors I was a whore?
I had crossed a line by scratching that itch, opened Pandora's Box, and I had no way to close it. It was too late, the damage already done. My dilemma now was what to do from here.

I rolled over and fell asleep suffering from a headache I'd created.

****

I guess the joke was on me because as soon as I got over my little 'bug' Sean went right back to being an inconsiderate asshole.

I should have known a problem of this magnitude wouldn't be solved that easy, *shit I could have caught a stomach bug a long time ago*!

I was beyond pissed, but I refused to fall back under Rell's spell, so I decided to keep his number blocked for the time being.

He had done nothing wrong, but I needed to solve my problem and I could no longer pacify myself using him as the resolution.

I was ready to confront Sean and tell him everything.

I prayed and prayed and the only thing that could set me free was the truth.

I wish I had found the strength to give Sean an ultimatum before I cheated.

It was killing me to just ignore his bullshit and harsh treatment, but for some reason it made me want to tell him even more what I had done, show him what his tactic lead me to do.

My actions were a direct result of his neglect.

I wanted his cocky arrogant ass to know that I wasn't as weak as he thought I was. I wasn't sitting around helpless, as he believed. I went out and found what I needed and it never would have happened if it wasn't for him treating me like shit all these years.

I think maybe a small part of me wanted him to hurt like he had hurt me for so long. Sean was my first and I wanted him to know I had given his loving away because he acted as if he no longer wanted it.

He needed to learn how to please and take care of me.

Really I just wanted Sean to care.

Nothing seemed to affect him, not one single tear that I cried got him to pay me any more attention.

Sometimes you don't appreciate something until it is gone. I wanted Sean to know that I was gone, so he'd realize he really wanted me to stay.

Yes I had gone outside of our marriage, but in going I realized that ultimately that's not what I wanted for my life, I wanted my husband and my family back and I was ready to re-commit mind, body and soul, but only if he was ready to re-commit as well.

I'd made my mind up, win or lose I was confessing, I just had to continue praying that God would show me how.

Chapter 10

I must have called this poor receptionist a million times trying to get through to Yolanda Young.

When I walked into the office the receptionist greeted me with a smile. She had no clue I was the woman who had harassed her all week.

"Good morning, how can I help you?" She asked politely. She was a cute girl who looked to be about in her early twenties.

"Yes, my name is Mariah Jones, and I have an appointment with Ms. Young."

"Perfect Mrs. Jones, she is expecting you, just go right in and I will sign you in, it is the last door on the right." She grabbed the sign in sheet from the other side of her desk and logged my name and the time I had arrived.

"Thank you." I said heading down the hall.

I peered through the door; I didn't want to just walk in so I tapped lightly.

"Come in Mariah, have a seat."

I walked over to her large dark cherry wood desk and took a seat. I placed my Michael Kors bag in the empty seat to my left.

She was pretty; she was actually very pretty, tall, light hair and brown eyes, she looked African American but she may have been mixed, it was hard to tell.

She sat so poised behind her desk; she wore black framed glasses and pearls. She had a traditional professional look to her, but any man could see she was a fox underneath the stiff suit.

There was something about her picture from the card that made me think she was who I needed to speak to. I guess that wouldn't be a good assessment since I hadn't even looked into anyone else. All I know is I didn't want someone who would judge me and since we were both sistas, maybe she'd be able to relate or at least have known someone in a similar situation.

I needed help and that is what I was here for.

"Good morning." I said softly, fidgeting in my seat, she was typing something in her laptop.

"It is not standard to give out individual counseling sessions."

She spoke in a soft almost monotone voice.

"I am what is known as a neutral mediator. However, you were very persistent, so, let's get right into what brings you in today. Ok?" She closed her laptop and smiled.

I took in a deep breath; this was going to be harder than I thought.

Regardless of how professional she looked, or how many degrees she had on the wall, she was still a stranger, and here I was getting ready to tell this stranger my darkest secret.

There is only one way to move forward Mariah and that is to take the first step, I told myself.

"Well.........from the outside looking in, everyone seems to think I have the perfect life. That is about 80% accurate, I do. I have a great life. I have a wonderful home, two beautiful boys and a wonderful provider as a husband, but Sean..." I was fidgeting with my wedding ring, I looked down at it, reminded by what it symbolized, "..my husband, he uuummmm...."

This was such a difficult thing to say out loud although I had practiced how this meeting would go, clearly I wasn't ready, but I needed to get ready because I was paying by the minute to be here.

"He doesn't please me sexually," I paused, waiting for her to clutch her pearls; she seemed unfazed so I just continued talking. "For years I've struggled with finding the right way to say this to him. I've tried everything; we've discussed it, I've written letters. When that didn't work I thought, ok, well maybe it must be me you know? So I tried to spice things up in the bedroom, you know add things to our sex life. I must have the entire bedroom Kandi collection!"

I finally took a breath. Somehow I felt better just getting it out. I noticed she wrote certain things down on a note pad. For some reason that made me nervous.

I thought about how I had gotten here, how messed up my marriage was and the even bigger mess I had made trying to solve it! I wished things could have gone differently. I wish Sean and I could've talked it out. I wish all the little things I had done would've worked.

I found myself thinking back to the time when I went out of my way trying to set the mood for us and he disregarded me, like I didn't even exist. What was on that phone that was more important than me?

I felt myself getting angry.

"I've stood right in front of him…….. it's like he doesn't even see me!"

I did not want to relive that moment. How devastating to be denied in such a way by your own husband?

Sensing my frustration, Yolanda looked up from her notes.

"Earlier you referenced this 80%," she looked back at her notes again, "so you're lacking 20%? Tell me, how did you deal with that void?"

"Well," I took a deep breath, "I went out and I got that itch scratched!"

She looked at me if she wanted more of an explanation, so I gave her one.

"I thought my problems would be solved, and initially they were. It was fun and exciting and I had no regrets," I though back over the years," and then I did. This isn't who I am, and honestly I am ashamed of the woman I've become." I admitted. "I couldn't imagine what my boys would think of me."

I held my head down in shame.

"People often times underestimate the importance of sexually satisfying their partners. Unfortunately I see marriages end all the time for this very reason."

At that moment I was glad that I made the choice to come here and open up. Yolanda seemed to understand that this was a real issue for me and I was here for a real resolution.

"I have to be completely honest with you Mariah." She had stopped writing and was now looking directly at me eye to eye. "What you've done have elevated things to a whole nother level."

I know this bitch didn't.......

"I know that I may have done the un-speak-able, but he pushed me to this!" I yelled in my defense, this had suddenly taken a turn in the wrong direction.

"There is blame to be placed on both sides, you are right," She was a little late with the reassurance. "But what resolution are you looking for at this point moving forward, that is the question?"

I had carried this load for too long, even before Rell, I was just tired and couldn't take another moment.

"I want to confess." I said.

"Confess?" Clearly I had taken her by surprise, the shock showed on her face.

"Yes! Maybe once he sees how far this has actually pushed me he will want to change! Maybe we can fix this problem and save the little piece of marriage we have left!"

".....and you believe, confessing to your husband that you've slept with another man is going to make him want to change?"

I guess that entire neutral mediator thing went out of the window once I had dropped this bomb on her, she seemed to be on Sean's side and she hadn't even met him!

I wanted to leave, but it was too late and I was in too deep. I had already confessed to her and she was going to help me from here whether she wanted to or not.

"I need you to help me find a way to confront my husband. I know this could go either way, but whatever the outcome is, I am ready to deal with it because it has got to be better than this hell I've been living in!"

Her formal training wouldn't allow her to interrupt me, but I could clearly see that she wanted to interject and clear up our misunderstanding, but I wasn't going to give her bougie ass a second to speak.

"Further, I didn't come here for your opinion, I came here for your expertise Ms. Young, are you going to help me or not?"

I sat back, crossed my arms and looked her dead in her eyes.

I left Ms. Yolanda Young's office 10 minutes later with an appointment scheduled for late next week, Thursday morning to be exact.

****

That night I went home and told my husband of nine years that I wanted a divorce.

I didn't really want a divorce but I needed his attention.

We had never discussed divorce during our entire marriage. While I had tried to tell him how unhappy I was throughout all the years, I had never taken it to this extreme.

Sean didn't speak to me for two days, on the third day his mother came over.

That was just like Sean to run to his mother instead of facing me himself.

I cannot understand why she enabled him, she should have sent him home to deal with his wife, instead she came to insert herself directly in the center of our marriage, but I had something for her too.

After 2 hours of being bricked walled she gave up and told Sean he'd better attend the session if he wanted to get to the bottom of what my problem was.

I did give in to one request of hers and agreed to let the boys go to her house while Sean and I figured out what was going on under our roof.

She insisted that her grandsons stay away from the cloud that I was causing in our home.

Whatever Bitch.

I was prepared for a full out war if that is what it took to get Sean to that session, it was best that the boys weren't here just in case something crazy happened.

For the remainder of the week we walked around the house not speaking to each other. I refused to give in.

All the years, I played the hand that was dealt. I kept quiet and portrayed the perfect family, well I was at my breaking point, the end of my rope.

It was easy for us to be upset at each other throughout the week with Sean's work schedule, but Sunday was a day that we usually spent in the house together, and we would be forced to speak at some point.

I was only interested in one conversation, and that was regarding our session scheduled for Thursday and getting him to agree to attend.

This hurt like hell and I had no one in my corner. Dawn and I had stopped communicating like we used to. I am not sure what was going on with that. Was Sean trying to create problems between us by doing small things to make me jealous?

Were they actually seeing each other behind my back? I couldn't imagine that, but you can't put anything past anyone now days. Shit, at least that would explain why my husband was so cold towards me!

Sean was stubborn as hell and I didn't know how much more of this I could take.

Tuesday morning, I decided that if I couldn't get this one small thing, than my marriage was already over and I was going to take the boys and go check into a hotel until I could figure things out.

I wouldn't be able to tell Sean that of course because he would use every last penny he had making sure he got custody of the boys.

This was spiraling out of control and the worst part about it was that Sean still hadn't said one word to me.

I was tired of being this a robot without a voice, tired of going through the motions like everything was fine when it wasn't. Tired of pretending to his friends and family that we had this picture perfect life because we didn't! I was tired of fucking another man to get the feeling my husband refused to give me!

I had allowed this man to take full control of my life and I didn't even realize it. I had isolated myself from my family, I couldn't even blame him for that, but he certainly supported my decision. Everything was his, the house, the cars, the money. I would have to fight him tooth and nail in court to get what I deserved. His mother and sister would run to his defense in an instant and I would have the fight of my life. He'd have his family to back him up and I would stand alone.

It was time to make a decision between my happiness or his money.

I fell asleep crying, again.

Thursday morning came way too soon. Sean and I still weren't speaking to each other.

I felt defeated. I had given all these years to this man and he wasn't even willing to give an hour to me! I don't know why I held on all this time.

I headed downstairs to make a pot of coffee and figure out my next move, Sean had clearly showed me where he stood.

The smell of coffee greeting me halfway down the stairs.

What the hell?

Sean was in the kitchen preparing breakfast!

I didn't know what to say, we hadn't spoken in almost a week, but even on the best of terms Sean didn't get up and prepare anything other than cereal for he and the boys occasionally.

"What time is the appointment?" he asked as if we were a regular couple.

"Uh, it is at um, 11:30. Sean wh......" I was shocked.

"I have to hop in the shower and shave, we'll leave at 11."

He walked past me without another word. I just stood there too stunned to say anything.

I wish I knew what he was thinking sometimes, but I didn't care, I was going to save my marriage and that was all that mattered!

EPILOGUE

We drove to the appointment in silence.

I was beyond nervous and anxious. I had no idea how this would end, I didn't even know how it would begin, but here I was, ready to face the music.

Sean was his usual self, distant and unresponsive; I had no idea what he was feeling. I was just happy that he agreed to attend the session.

It was hard to get a reaction from him; he was so calm and poised all the time. I don't think I had ever heard him use a curse word. I wondered what type of reaction he would have to my confession.

I couldn't remember the last time Sean and I were in the same car together, we stopped pretending that we enjoyed each other's company long ago, now we were together, driving to a marriage counselor's office that I had hired to assist me in confessing to him that I had slept with another man behind his back.

Someone should make a book about my life, I thought to myself reflecting my entire situation.

My mother always would say the truth is stranger than fiction, I now know what she meant.

The second we got in the car Sean turned the radio up, an indicator that he did not want to talk, which was fine with me.

He listened to old school Anita Baker, she was singing about the sweetest love and I wondered how a man so out of touch with his wife could even listen to love songs, he was so far from romantic, but the way he sang made me think otherwise.....

We pulled into the office parking lot as I swallowed a large lump in my throat, it was too late to back out now.

I sat in the passenger seat waiting for Sean to open my door.

I stepped out of his Mercedes and grabbed my bag as Sean closed the door.

"Lead the way." He said.

We headed towards the sliding double doors and in the elevator up to the 3rd floor.

I hadn't noticed before but the building was actually very discreet. There were no large signs advertising their services. I guess when you are having marital issues you appreciate the privacy, I know I did.

We stepped off the elevator and were immediately greeted by Ms. Young's bubbly assistant.
"Good morning Mrs. Jones, how are you today?"

"Good thank you. We have an appointment with Ms. Young this morning."

"Absolutely! I have you right here." She highlighted my name on a list containing appointments. "I signed you in already, but I will need the gentleman to sign in."

Sean was standing next to me cool as a cucumber.

"Where do I sign Miss?"

"I got it hun," I was stalling for time, "you can head on down to the office, right there, and it'll be the last door on your left."

Miss Bubbly was on the phone discretely speaking to a client.

I signed Sean's name, took a deep breath and headed down the corridor.

I was about three feet away from Ms. Young's office door when I heard what seemed to be talking inside.

The door was open and the conversation was heard clear as day.

"Sean?! Hey baby. How did you.... what are you doing here?" Nervous laughter followed.

Everything slowed down.

I closed my eyes and tried to blink away the reality in front of me, I grabbed the frame of the door for stability, I felt weak in my knees.

Never in a million years would I have thought things would turn out this way.

In no way am I claiming victim, because I know what I've done. I mean, that's why we were here but I was trying to make it right. I knew we had a serious problem and I was ready to face it and honestly work towards a resolution to save my marriage.

I thought I had it all figured out. I'd confess, he'd forgive me and recognize all the things he didn't do, all my needs he didn't fulfill and make it right, because he didn't want to lose me.

I was his wife, the mother of his children.

I was not prepared for this, and I was not able to formulate enough thought to say a word.

I stood there faced with the realization that the man I was trying to convince to stay was already gone.

I starred directly into her face, rage burning through my skin.

I tried to make a rational decision. I tried to think the situation through.

Just to be clear, I'm from the streets, the very bottom, but I educated myself and sought out a different life style. I married well and never had to look back.

I guess that old saying was true, you can take the girl out the hood, but you can't take the hood out the girl……….. It was like the devil himself was begging me to show these two what I was made of.

In a matter of seconds, that seemed more like hours, all the pieces of the puzzle came together and suddenly it all made sense.

The card that I thought was his sisters had actually fallen from his pockets! My husband was having an affair with our marriage counselor!

Here I was thinking I had done him so wrong, wishing that I had found another way to get through to him, regretting the moments that I'd spent with Rell and this bastard was fucking someone else the entire time!

I had come here at my lowest point, feeling like scum and the bitch that I'd confessed my deepest darkest secrets to was the same bitch my husband was fucking!

Did she know he was married?

Did she know me all along?

Did she know it was MY husband she was fucking?

Sean stood there looking at her with a look of pure stupidity on his face, actually they both looked shocked.

They had no idea I was standing right there.

He was caught and I was about to catch a case!

I slowly took two steps into the room and closed and locked the door behind me.

I grabbed the large vase of white roses from the table by the door; my husband had probably bought them any fucking ways and I tossed the entire thing across the room causing a large crash with the shattering of the glass.

They were lost in their own personal moment, but I had their attention now.

"BABY?!? I know damn well you did not just call my husband baby! SEAN, HOW THE FUCK DO YOU KNOW HER?"

Sadly I already knew what was going on here, I just wanted him to admit it, so I could commit to this ass kicking.

"Ok, how about everyone just calm down."

That bitch was trying to be in control but I could tell by her expression she was scared to death.

On the other side of the door Miss Bubbly was trying to get in and help her Boss, I was sure she didn't know what had happened but any fool could see where this was going.

Once she realized she was locked out I heard her frantic voice calling 911.

At this point I didn't give a fuck, they would sure need them, and the way I saw it, they still had to get here and by then, I'd have my answers.

"CALM DOWN? Bitch miss me with that neutral mediator bullshit, because what you don't know is that I am two seconds off your ass!"

"Mariah!"

"And don't you Mariah me you son of a bitch, because there ain't shit you can say! I heard both of you talking you fucking bastard! How do you think we ended up here? You think this is a coincidence? I found her card last year in our laundry room, from one of your pockets! Thinking it was your sisters from her messy ass marriage, I came here trying to fix us! I thought, shit, if she can save them maybe she could help us too, and the whole time I was wrong! Your fucking the bitch I am confiding in!" I was screaming at the top of my lungs.

"There is no need for the name calling Mariah."

This bitch had the nerve to be offended cause I called her a bitch?

That was it; I lunged across that desk on her ass. I was tired of seeing her face and hearing her voice.

I grabbed a handful of her fake ass blonde hair and pulled her down until I was banging her big ass forehead on her desk. Once I had her down that was it!

I took my other hand and gave her a solid uppercut and then another one and another one……

"BITCH-I-WILL-FUCKING-KILL-YOU-YOU-HOME-WRECKING-WHORE!" I was spelling out this ass whooping, another punch for each word!

"SEEEAAAANNNNN!" She screamed.

Sean? Sean? This hoe was calling MY husband to save her.

Oh yeah the joke was on me, but this ass whooping would be on the house, free of charge!
When I felt a hand around the back of my neck, my heart broke on another level. Here I was dragging this hoe, as she deserved, as she screamed for my man to help her and here he was, actually trying to help HER?

Oh hell to the no!

They were jumping me! My husband and his HOE!!!

I was reaching for anything I could get my hands on, I needed a weapon cause I was going to kill Sean!

He picked her side in that moment and it was now 2 against 1.

I somehow found a metal three-hole punch and as Sean pulled me off her I came up swinging, straight for his head!

He put his arm up just in time to block the blow; I hit his arm causing a nasty gash that began to bleed immediately. Good! I'll whoop both their asses!

I was seeing red!

"YOU BITCH!"

I snapped out of my trance.

"What?" My chest rose and fell rapidly as I tried to catch my breath.

"You heard me, look at you! You're a fucking animal! I should have left you where I found you!"

Sean may have been the king of rude but he never disrespected me. It was my turn to have the stupid look on my face.

"Don't stand there looking stupid Mariah!" It's obvious neither of us have been happy. What did you think was going on? I haven't touched you! I have no desire to! I've kept you around this long because of my boys. You think my Mom hates you, she is the one who convinced me to stay and try to make it work!"

"Sean!" Yolanda pleaded with him.

I had just smashed her face in yet even she felt sorry for the way Sean was handling me.

"You shut the fuck up Bitch!" I tried to go after her again, but Sean wasn't having it.

143

"Mariah, it's over. Whatever you brought me here for, save it, because it's irrelevant. I'm filing for a divorce and custody of my kids."

"Sean, don't you think she's been through enough for today?"

I heard Yolanda talking to him, but I couldn't respond. Sean wanted a divorce and to take the boys?

I stood there starring at the white roses all over the floor.

"Mariah.... listen, I had no idea that......ah...... I was not aware that Sean was your husband. I was not aware that Sean was married at all!" Although I wasn't looking at her, from her tone that last statement was directed to Sean. "I would never conduct myself in such a way. Sean has never been here, to my office I mean. I was just as shocked as you..., I mean, well maybe not as shocked as you but......."

Bang, bang, bang, bang!

We all jumped.

"POLICE, OPEN UP!"

"She's hurting her, break it down, hurry, there was glass and screaming!" I heard the receptionist crying.

One good hit and the door was open and three officers rushed inside, two males and one female.

The two male officers immediately grabbed me and held me in a restraint.

One of the officers grabbed my arms and cuffed my hands behind my back. I couldn't even speak.

"Ma'am, would you like to press charges?" The female Officer was asking Yolanda, she and Sean were bleeding and it was clear I was the culprit.

She looked up at the Officer and then to Sean, who slowly nodded his head yes.

I tried as hard as I could to break free but those Officers had me cuffed, but I still tried to break free!

"Wait, NO! Sean! SEAN!!!" They literally had to drag me out of that office and it took the both of them too!

SEEAAAANNNNN!" I screamed as I was led to the elevator.

This shit ain't over!

Also by Author Celeste Celeste

When three college friends unite for a fun-filled weekend it's just like old times. Old friends and new coming together for a beautiful beach front wedding. But when the deck is shuffled and cards are dealt these friends will have a parallel clash that just may destroy them forever.

Will their friendship be able to survive this revelation or will it set in motion a fatal finale?

Three of a Kind is a juicy page turner that promises to have you on the edge of your seat, yearning for more!

Celeste Celeste is also the CEO of the brand and online boutique High Maintenance, where you can purchase paperback copies of Three of a Kind, Scratch Scratch

Log on and check it out **www.highmaintenance1.com**

To contact the Author email; authorcelesteceleste@gmail.com